A R HOLMES

PHARAOH

POWER BEHIND THE SUN

ASH Brothers Group, LLC, *Publishers*
Copyright © 2020 Antoine Ruffin Holmes All rights reserved

First edition, 2020 / Design by Antoine Holmes

Cover design by: Antoine Holmes
ISBN 978-0-578-71402-8 (Paperback)

To Asia—
who inspired me to write this story

&

To Monica—
who sacrificed everything to give me this chance

Praise of Re Har-akhti, Rejoicing on the Horizon, in His Name as Shu Who Is in the Aten-disc, living forever and ever; the living great Aten who is in jubilee, lord of all that the Aten encircles, lord of heaven, lord of earth, lord of the House of Aten in Akhet-Aten

The King of Upper and Lower Egypt, who lives by Maat, the Lord of the Two Lands: Nefer-kheperu-Re Wa-en-Re; the Son of Re, who lives on truth, the Lord of Diadems: Akh-en-Aten, long in his lifetime

The Chief Wife of the King, his beloved, the Lady of the Two Lands: Nefer-neferu-Aten Nefertiti, living, healthy, and youthful forever and ever; the Fan-Bearer on the Right Hand of the King...

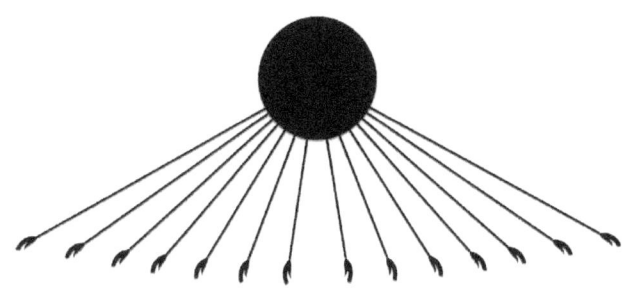

PROLOGUE

MY THOUGHTS.

I'm thinking as I sit here listening. I control all that is said and will be decided around this table of the priests. They conspire, but the conspiracy is of my doing. The threat of losing everything burns behind my passions as I remember the glory days I prayed I would see once more. I fix my posture into the wooden gold platted chair to sit a little closer to the conversation. We will create fear, but I am the one to be feared. The air is thick with heat, making beads of sweat drip down my bald head and back, from the poorly vented dark chamber room hidden within the hypostyle hall we are in. I will not be passed over, not this time.

He betrayed me, he had countless opportunities not to do it—

He needs to *die*.

The chamber room is lighted by candles in corners, with one candle which sits in the middle of the table. I pull the wax light closer with one hand and smack the table with the other. The priests silenced themselves, giving all their attention to the head of the table where I sit.

"It's crucial that what is said here is to never be said outside this room." All the priests nod their heads in understanding and obedience. The room is silent. I stare at them, looking for any challenging behavior.

There is none.

I clap my hand once to give the signal…

"Continue!"

They converse. The table of brown faces talk over each other, all are looking for dominance.

I watch.

I listen.

"*Panehesy.*"

I hear my name being called. It does not come from the table. I look around and notice some movement towards the back of the room down a smaller dark corridor. I leave the table and walk unsure and slowly forward, becoming very *submissive and humble* to a tall sizeable stranger that is standing in the shadows.

My thoughts slow, I am terrified.

The stranger having a mysterious like presence kept its appearance hidden from me with a black hooded cloak.

I'm fearful of looking up. I hesitate but slowly lift my head to stare into its dark hood—

The towering shadowy figure bends over towards me and whispers. The language is of a strange slithering sound. A dialect unrecognizable to most, but I understand it. The hiss becomes louder, louder, and louder until it stops. The figure turns its head very fast towards the entrance of the sanctuary and sees a priest holding a candle standing looking upon us without distress or submission.

I notice the distraction, but before I could acknowledge the priest, the hooded figure races towards the standing priest at the entrance. The speed of the hooded figure is so fast that the priests around the table did not see the giant figure racing by them. Trailing behind it was darkness, which filled the room, overcoming any present light.

There is silence.

The room is dark and quiet.

With a trembling hand, I light a candle and walk towards the table of the priests. They all look at me with confusion.

My eyes bulge filled with water from anxiety.

I stare at the entrance of the sanctuary. There is nothing but a lit candle on the floor.

The hooded figure and the priest are gone...

BOOK ONE: PHARAOH
CHAPTER ONE
QUEEN TIY

KEMET, AKHETATEN – ROYAL COURTYARD
THE EARLY MORNING WIND whistles through the courtyard as the pure sound of a child's laughter fills the yard. A beautiful, yet very old in age woman, sits on a chair wearing a light yellowish cotton gown embroidered with accents of gemstones around the neckline, watches a young boy playing nearby. The woman of dark brown complexion and beauty is the Royal Great Wife and Queen of King Amenhotep III — Queen Tiy.

Sitting looking at the young boy, I smile proudly.

The wind blows through my afro styled hair and down my body. It catches the bottom of my gown, making it move gracefully, dancing to its own rhythm. The young boy looks over to me, smiles, and continues to play.

My grandson, Prince Tutankhaten.

"Tut…Tut. Come here… come here, son… sit down."

The young prince walks over to me, leans over, kisses my forehead, and sits down at my feet.

"I love you — do you know — "

Tut looks up at me and smiles.

"Do you know who you are?"

"Do you know the importance of this family, this dynasty?"

Young Tut sits there with his mouth open, wanting to speak but speechless. He looks confused a little, but curious to what I will say next.

"You need to know the truth... about Kemet... its *essence*, it's *power*, it's *love*, and it's *legacy*!"

"The truth?" Young Tut says quietly.

"Yes, the truth!" I continue. "Kemet is the heart of the world, everything and everyone strives to be it —

"The Nile is our vein that pumps the life, which gives that black vibrant color of divinity.

"This is the Essence!

"The Divine touched us first!

"The temples, the Pyramids, the Sphinx… you see… this all around you… even the gold that you wear is from this land. This is Power! The Divine has fashioned us with Royalty —

"With all these splendors, do you not see the love? Creation itself is love."

Young Tut sits eyes large, waiting to hear more.

"For the first time in all of Kemet, this Dynasty recognizes the divinity of its women. I am the King's Great Royal Wife. His love for me can move heaven and earth. Before me, the women of this Dynasty — your family were venerated with this high esteem. But is this enough..."

"What do you mean... is that enough?" said young Tut. "All that you have mentioned shows me so much. I am blessed by Aten to be a part of this legacy."

I soften my voice and lean over. "I understand, and I don't want to taint your view, but there are things... crucial things that you need to know. Your time as the Pharaoh is coming soon."

Young Tut stood and shouted, "As Pharaoh... Now! What about —"

I grab him and look across the yard. "Stop! Listen — don't say anything right now. I need you to listen."

"We don't have much time! You need to understand that while Aten is the resident God here in Akhetaten, it is not the same in all of Kemet.

"I want so much for the understanding and worship of Aten to be. They say Amen moves in mysterious ways, but *we* know there's nothing mysterious about the Aten. Amen was and still is the resident God of Kemet and with this Thutmoseid Dynasty. There are other entities besides the works of the Amen priesthood that are at odds with us. The heart of Kemet is changing again!"

"Again," says the young prince, puzzled as he sits down to the ground.

"Yes!" I said sorrowfully.

"For the first time in Kemet, foreign invaders attacked us. These northern conquerors were called the Hyksos. They destroyed our essence, our own identity, and our heart."

With the gentle touch, a grandmother gives her grandchild, I lean forward caressing his face and rubbing his cheeks.

"With this, Kemet suffered its greatest humiliation—" I said, leaning back into my chair and closing my eyes.

This is our story.

Our history.

Our war.

CHAPTER TWO
KING AHMOSE

KEMET, MEDJAY TRAINING QUARTERS: TA-APET (THEBES) – CITY OF THE AMEN

THE SOUND OF SPEARS CRACKS against one another as swords whistle through the air as they hit. Nubian dark complexion men train with weapons and hand to hand combat. A medium-built man walks into the entrance of the training quarters and stands within the shadows. He is a dark and intense man in his early twenties.

I am Commander General *King Ahmose*.

They are my men, they are my Medjay.

They are men with duties to ensure the safety of my citizens and their property. They police the frontier region of my country from invaders. They *must* be ready. They *must* be an example for my military.

I watch it from a distance. I didn't want the men to see me and get distracted. However, it's time to see what they have learned.

A small group of fifty men trains towards the western wall. Some notice me, but most are unaware of my presence as I walk towards them.

"Assemble your men four rows!" I say to them as I approach closer.

The men come together.

One continues to sit, watching underneath a tented area. The tented area is so dark that I almost didn't notice anyone sitting there. The men, young and old, rush to create the formation. The seated man stands and walks toward us.

He bows his head towards me.

The men recognize him and fix their posture and stick out their chests and showed fear on their faces. This is the "Charioteer of The Residence," General Pennekheb, who is a great swordsman, and one of my trusted officers.

"As Medjay and soldiers, we are sworn to protect the King, his family, and keep law and order in Kemet," Pennekheb yells out. "Before we can do that, we must know ourselves and what we are capable of."

He looks at the men at the beginning of each row. He continues his rant as he stares them down as if he was looking at their souls.

"To understand the supernatural self of man and his soul, one should study and not just follow the unseen principles of the creator but overstand it. To have an overstanding of things allows you to see it more in-depth. This means these hidden principles of this force that exist in life also live in man.

"To have knowledge of self, it will reveal itself to you, and also the laws that govern the material and spiritual aspects of the universe—" Pennekheb continues.

Pennekheb walks up and down each row and looks at the men as he passes.

"—our unique fighting styles are not just movements but are animalistic. The *NTCHR* is the unseen principle of the God's, which embodies nature. Understanding this is the key to our success.

"*Heru*, the Falcon, king of the rising and setting sun and master of the skies that overlook the earth. It can gaze directly at the sun, the light... *the truth*, which man must do to look at oneself. The truth to everything is within!"

He walks to the end of the rows and turns around to head back but stands there behind them.

"*Jhuty*, the Ibis Crane, the heart and tongue of Ra, who is the scribe of the forces of nature. This is a soft and gentle but deadly fighting style that shows the awesome power of being calm and still. The ability to remain motionless for a long time—

"*Natchet*, the Snake, was always feared for its power, force, and its keen sense of feelings. It can determine danger by the vibrations on the ground, and it could stop almost any enemy with its lethal strike—this is what you need to become!" He continues as he begins to walk toward the front of the ranks.

"*Enpu*, the Black Jackal, the master of transformation. He leads you to the scales of truth, existing in the *Duat*, the Afterworld. He is guardian and protector of the balance of judgment, and opener of roads, leading to both celestial or terrestrial universes."

Pennekheb stops at the head of the rows, look at them and pulls out a black cloth and ties it around his eyes. Using the Jhuty fighting style, he stands on one leg and challenges them.

"In knowing this, if you think you can strike me — *strike me!*" Pennekheb shouts.

The first two soldiers from each row formed a circle around the general and charged him. The general used the fighting styles and the arts to defeat them without being hit. Two of the men were using hand to hand combat techniques while the other two were trying to use kicking techniques.

He combined the *Jhuty* technique with *Natchet*, utilizing agility and the vibrations from the ground and the energy of each movement from the men to block every kick and punch.

The other rows cheered along, some look to join the fight and others with the look of relief that they weren't called upon.

"Give the general a challenge and give the men some weapons," I said to the instructors.

The first two rows move out of the way since they were mostly on the ground. The others with weapons charged him, as the general applies the fighting style of the *Heru*. Using the method of sight and looking right through the black cloth, he sees their aura and every move they make before they did it.

Patiently and effortlessly, the general defeats them.

One of the men has a hard surface thick stick and strikes the general in the back. As the weapon hits him, it catches nothing but sandy brownish air because Pennekheb was nowhere to be seen, leaving the men confused and puzzled.

The men noticed movement under the tent where the general was sitting before the beginning of the training.

In the depth of the shadows, you see the general sitting there as if he never got up.

He stands to his feet and walks to the men.

"When and how did I beat you all?"

"Was it, now or when I got up the first time —" Pennekheb yells to the men.

" — or did I even get up at all?"

I signal them to get up because some of the men were still on the ground

"The technique I used was a special technique used only by trained assassins, skilled priest and the King—it is only used if necessary," Pennekheb continues.

I move closer to Pennekheb and tap him on the shoulder. He nodded to me, which gave a signal to him that I am taking over the conversation.

Pennekheb steps back as I moved forward.

"The mind is the greatest weapon—" I said.

"You can defeat any opponent if you believe you can. If the mind becomes weak, then it can be easily controlled as well. The *NTCHR* taught the overstanding of *Ma'at*, the feminine qualities that represent the universal laws of cosmic order, harmony, balance, and equilibrium. *Ma'at* governs all *NTCHR* and men... Therefore, we must help to liberate our lands from any foreign control that will move us away from that principle.

"Without this, chaos reigns unchecked, and the ability to create order is forever lost."

I grab a wooden staff from one of the men, prepared to use it until I recognize one of my royal servants entering the training area. He walks swiftly and whispers to an instructor. As the servant stands there waiting, the instructor walks to another high-ranking soldier, Lieutenant Crew Commander, Ahmose, son of Abana.

Ahmose looks at the servant, then gives his attention to the instructor and nods. As he walks over to me, he glances over to First Sergeant Ameni, giving him a signal to prepare the men.

"Pardon me, my Lord," Ahmose says quietly. "There is word from the north that the Hyksos army has left Avaris and is heading towards Thebes."

"General Pennekheb, come with me. Lieutenant Ahmose, send word to the royal court that we are leaving Thebes. Then have your officers regroup with the men surrounding the city and meet me at the first post." I said to Ahmose as Pennekheb walks over to us.

As Pennekheb and I exit the training area, you hear Ahmose in the background giving orders and preparing the men for battle against the Hyksos.

CHAPTER THREE
KING AHMOSE

*THE WAR OF OUR FATHERS: SHARUHEN –
SOUTHERN PALESTINE OUTSKIRTS*
TWILIGHT

THE MIGHTY WAR CHARIOTS tower over my foot soldiers. Chariots from the elite Asar Regiment—a division of my Army—move the lightweight machines into position.

I walk between them.

We've been fighting for days. Exhausted and covered with blood and sand I walk laboriously and slowly towards the front of the line with Ahmose, and Pennekheb.

"You might as well walk right up to their horses and ask it to leave," Ahmose says to me.

"These shepherds would never leave," Pennekheb interrupts. "They are too close to their own land than to just leave it to us. I do despise their nature but admire their determination."

We reached the front of the line.

Superb martial preparations are underway. The chariots join twenty-five other units.

Archers are taking up the position. The long-range composite bows for killing at a distance are being loaded.

Infantry soldiers are also preparing their penetrating axes and sickle-swords.

My lieutenants and I stare down from the sandy hilltop.

In the distance is the Hyksos encampment, our enemy.

"They just will not submit!" Ahmose shouts.

"They have submitted. I'm just going to remind them that they have already been overthrown…," I interrupted, gazing down at the Hyksos position.

"At my first signal, destroy them all. We'll use the chariots to smash the enemy formations by shock."

"My King, I don't think that is wise—

—our chariots might be hit when the arrows come down," Pennekheb says, his commanding voice lessening my command.

"I hope they are accurate because I'm going to be in front," I said, quickly staring down at the enemy. "This hik-khase should know they're already dead."

Ahmose and I reach the bottom of the hilltop. The chariots of two hundred Asar Regiment warriors are directly behind us in battle formation.

Sweat drips from their faces. They wait as a light sandy wind blows through the battlefield— the Hyksos position can be seen across the sandy terrain.

I give the nod to one of my men.

The charioteer rides to the side of the hill and nods to a foot soldier waiting.

Pennekheb is at the top of the hill. The four hundred archers of the Asar Regiment are loaded and waiting behind him. He sees the nod of the foot soldier from the charioteer from below.

"Now!" Pennekheb shouts.

The mighty bows are released. The archers fire a murderous barrage of piercing arrows.

The screaming is almost proximate. We watch as the arrows strike down into the Hyksos camp. The fatal rain of piercing arrows sends panic through the base camp.

"Hold position... wait...", I yell. I see the confusion of the camp continuing — another wave of arrows is released — they panic. Herds of Hyksos begin to flee across the sandy terrain.

I whisper praise to the God Amen —

I inhale a sharp breath and raise my sickle-sword.

"Soldiers of Kemet — take your final revenge! For Justice! For Peace! For *Tawi*!" I shouted.

The men cheer and stomp their feet on the floor of their chariots. They race from the bottom of the hilltop towards the fleeing hundreds of Hyksos...

I lead the terrifying and ruthless chariot charge. At my side is the Asar Regiment as they shout out fearsome war cries as they move across the rough sandy plain toward the Hyksos. Arrows are crashing down everywhere around us.

"*Amen*," I breathe.

The chariots smash into the Hyksos at full speed—it is butchery. The Asar Regiment charioteers slash mercilessly with their sickle swords, cutting a path of pure destruction through the enemy.

The Hyksos, however, fought with equal brutality. Struggling with their own chariots and foot soldiers, they pull, shoot (using bow and arrow), and speared my soldiers off their chariots whenever they could.

I turn my chariot and throw my sword with expert efficiency and cut the heads off two Hyksos archers. Before their bodies hit the ground, a spear from a different location stabs through the neck of my horse.

Before I decapitated them, two arrows were released from the falling archers and hit the middle of my horse's body as it collapses forward. My chariot buckled and flipped over my dead horse's head as it crashes to the sandy ground.

Crawling from underneath my chariot, I'm amid the battle. It takes everything in me to stand, not to fall and give in to my enemy.

I can barely breathe.

The ground trembles as my Asarian foot soldiers charge down the hill towards the battlefield. A thunderous roar shrieks through the air. The cry grows louder and louder in its approach. Half of my men charge the remaining Hyksos at the camp and the other half towards my charioteers and me.

No fear for death, I stand.

Proving my impeccable worth as a warrior — I slashed and dodge — escaping near death at every turn. I scream a passionate roar of rage as I fight for my life. Until — they surround me from all sides.

"The hell you waiting for?" I yelled. "Get on with it!"

More of my men still fight in the distance. The ones closer to me that was struggling at my side are all dead.

A tall wounded Hyksos man walks towards me, pushing pass his men. He is higher in rank than the men that surround me — A general maybe…

"You're done," the Hyksos general says. "Drop your weapon. Now!"

Sweat mixed with blood and sand pour down my face. They will have to kill me before I surrender. My heart beats so loud it drowns out the general's commands to me. Every part of my body screams with strain.

I will not die today.

Before I start to make my final attack, I see them — my men.

The foot soldiers slash their way through the Hyksos and slaughter several of them around me. The Hyksos general charges towards me, raising his arm to cut. I rushed towards him and slid to the ground, slashing his groin upward through his stomach. His eyes widen in horror and pain when he drops…

They are beaten!

In the distance, a young man, a scribe, stares down at the field. He watches as the Asar Regiment below concludes the battle. Ahmose gets in his chariot and rides towards him. The Regiment cheers as the last isolated pockets of Hyksos are cut down. He goes to the bottom of the hilltop and looks up at the young man.

"Did you see it all," Ahmose calls.

"Yes, master! I have written down everything!" He yells.

I find a man-less chariot and ride towards them. Both men greeted me with a nod.

"My King," Ahmose says, nodding.

I greeted them by taking my right hand, making a fist, and crossing my body with it touching my left chest.

"This day, I swear to Tawi, no foreigner will rule our lands while my dynasty rules. I give my word, in this life and the next, I will protect her. All the praise is to Amen-Ra, for he is merciful," I exhaled.

I turn back to the battlefield —
"These are my words — let them be written!"

***

IT IS A GRAND VIEW OF THEBES seen from the stairs of the Royal Palace. My soldiers and the Medjay line the streets while the people cheer. The Amen priest stands at the steps of the Royal Palace, as the Queen, Ahmose-Nefertari, and I enter riding in a chariot surrounded by more Medjay. Governor's, Vizier's, and all of Kemet royalty welcome my return.

The chariot comes to a halt at the steps of the palace, two servants of the royal house help us out. My Queen walks beside me as the noise from the crowd stops. They fall silent and bow down to greet us as we reach the top of the stairs. I turn around and take my Queen's hand, raising it up towards the sky in celebration.

Unknowing to me, one of the Amen priests stands near a column behind us, watching us, as the crowd below cheer in celebration. Out from the darkness, a large greenish-gray, scaly hand touches the shoulder of the priest. Despite the celebration below, the priest bows to the stranger and points into my direction.

Keeping its appearance hidden and the rest of its body in the shadows. They walk away into the darkness of the palace.

CHAPTER FOUR
QUEEN TIY
NEW KINGDOM

AKHETATEN   –   ROYAL   COURTYARD
I ALWAYS ENJOY these walks with my grandson.

He runs over to a table where a servant is laying out a mid-day meal for us. It's high noon and silent in the courtyard. The nostalgias and peace of the old ways are what he needs to learn — before it's his time to take the throne.

"Oh... there is so much to know with so little time. Did you understand the story I just told you?" I start.

"I did —" Tut answers with food in his mouth. "I understood... I heard some of these stories before about King Ahmose and the invaders but not like this. I see the stories on the walls, they are told to me at bedtime." He turns and looks at me as I walk over.

"Sometimes they don't seem real, as if it didn't really happen... but it was an amazing story!" Tut finishes.

I sit down beside him and inhale the clean, brisk air. "Well, baby, the truth is what you will hear from me. It's so important for you to know and understand these things." I continued.

I notice my servants were gone and that Tut and I were alone. Sipping out of my cup, I lean a little closer to him.

"There is more to know... so you finish up your food and pay close attention," I whispered.

I begin this story with views of the expansion of Kemet through its wealth and monumental building projects. The growth and power we wielded over time assisted us in being the most revered kingdom on earth.

"Your Great, Great Grandfathers went to great lengths to maintain and expand this empire. They took expeditions through swamps of the Euphrates, and the deep south, Kush—Nubia."

I lean back and smile as he sits here, so engaged with me. His eyes full, mouth partly open, waiting for me to continue.

"There was a ruler of great importance, who was different and extraordinary in many ways...," I continued.

"First, because of great aptitude."

"Second, because she was a woman."

Tut mouth drops. He moves timidly toward me. "A woman!" Tut yells.

"Yes, a woman," smiling at his curiosity, "This is your Great, Great Grandmother—Queen Hatshepsut, the Great Royal Wife of King Thutmose II."

"Close your eyes," I said to Tut as I take the cup out of his hands. "Now sit back, listen, and see."

***

THEBES – MIDDAY

A YOUNG BOY walks towards the temple. He is wearing shoulder garments that are wrapped around the upper torso covering the chest and shoulders. The clothing is covered with fine gold and laced in turquoise ornaments going in straight lines three rows around the upper body. The stomach is visible, and his biceps are covered with arm bracelets made of gold. The torso down to the lower part of the knee is covered with a white cotton wrap. His feet covered with gold-laced sandals that have one strap that goes over the top of the foot at the base of the leg. He is proud and strong in stature. He is Prince Thutmose III—

Young Prince Thutmose III gets closer to the temple. Ineni, an important counselor who serves his stepmother, Queen Hatshepsut, meets him midway and walks with him.

"You are late, young Prince? We have been planning this for days now," said Ineni.

"A lot is going on that you are unaware of." Thutmose III says while looking at Ineni with resentment but keeping his composure around him. "Your Queen, Hatshepsut has done well not bringing the issue to you, but she doesn't like your service to me, and she wishes for me not to rule."

Ineni cuts his eye at the prince...

"She is against this coregency with me," said Thutmose III.

"The Queen brings to me only what she wants or needs of my council. I serve you out of choice and out of respect for your father, may the Gods continue to watch over him and that he rests in peace." Ineni says quietly.

Thutmose III turns his attention away from Ineni. "Very well. I apologize. Don't take my frustration as a personal attack. Nehesi and the others are plotting against me." He says softly. "I'm sure of it."

"What? I... I haven't..." Ineni says surprisingly.

"It's... OK! I know you must have heard something," Thutmose III interjects, as they get closer to the temple of Amen.

"Just keep your eyes open. The council will be watching you." Ineni responds, keeping his tone flat as they stop in front of the temple.

They pause at the entrance, looked at one another then entered. A tall, athletic built Nubian greets the young men as they enter the temple. One of Queen Hatshepsut's most trusted lieutenants, Chancellor Nehesi.

"Peace be unto you, young Prince. Your Queen is waiting." Nehesi says, smiling as he greets the prince.

With no response, Thutmose walks past Nehesi and enters a more massive courtyard that is surrounded by royalty, the Queen's principal counselors, administrators, viziers, and Amen priest. Halfway to the center, he turns his head slightly to the right to see Queen Hatshepsut, a full figure brown-skinned woman sitting on a six-step gold and ivory chair. He also notices an empty golden chair beside her with two dark-skinned Nubian Medjay bodyguards closely behind.

The Queen nods to Thutmose, acknowledging him, and he returns it back. At that moment, the sun sits high above, sending its rays down through the temple shining on the Queen. She stands and says —

"Today, before the presence of Ra and all Kemet, I join this union with Thutmose III. May Amen bless this unification that it will be accepted in their presence." Queen Hatshepsut starts as she looks towards the direction of the Amen priest.

"With this union, I form this coregency — come and sit upon the throne." She continues, turning her attention to her administrators. "So, shall it be written, so shall it be done…"

***

"WAIT," young Tut interrupts. "I thought you said, she ruled alone."

"She did rule… She had to share it with her step-son first," I said immediately. "Thutmose III was very young when the king died, so Hatshepsut became a co-regent and ruled right alongside him — for only a short period…" I continued.

I quickly look around. Not that what I'm saying shouldn't be said but for my servants that are nearby. I stand and walk away but close enough for Tut to hear me.

"With the rule of Queen Hatshepsut and now this coregency Kemet became an imperial power…"

A moment of hesitation runs through me, frustrated with the traditions of how things were usually done. I turn to face him to make sure he is listening.

"Remember, all the customs and rituals were fashioned towards the rule of men kings up to this point…"

Tut looks up at me with a slight smile. His expression so lively and innocent it's infectious. Even I find myself grinning as I continue…

"You know the land and the people. You can see how things are governed… Hatshepsut had to go through great lengths to tell her story. Across the Nile from Thebes, into the barren valleys of the desert… Against the cliffs lies a masterpiece of architecture. Try to image it —

"The temple laid out on three terraces approached by ramps. The center and main terrace avenue lead to an entrance that is lined with Sphinxes. The forecourt holds a sacred boat shrine. This is her temple. The walls show scenes where she was conceived by the God Amen and the high points of her life reigning as King…

"She was known by some as a weak ruler because she did little to expand our empire. But during the coregency, Thutmose expanded the empire through military campaigns while Hatshepsut maintained the royal authority at home. She alone sent to the land of Punt one of the greatest trading expeditions known to Kemet —"

For a moment, I can almost see it... Large vessel fleet ships ported being filled by servants and the King of Punt's servants. In the distance, I can see Queen Hatshepsut meeting with the King of Punt negotiating the cargo. The King, giving Kemet their riches which were, myrrh trees, frankincense, ebony, pure ivory, iron, gold, apes, monkeys, dogs, leopard skins, and natives all from the land of Punt.

"Let it be known that during Queen Hatshepsut's reign, she ruled Kemet fairly and firmly," I finished while shuffling Tut over to an open fountain. I release a deep breath and gaze at the water flowing around the outer panels pouring down to a basin. Water fills my eyes... My hand wades the stream from the pool as I watch Tut walk down to the far end playing with a small wooden model of a ship in it.

"Love," I said softly over the pouring sound of the fountain.

"What? What did you say, grandma?" Tut yells, walking back towards me.

"I mentioned earlier about Kemet's love," I said, taking my hands out of the water and shaking them against the cool breeze to dry. "Love is what keeps this land growing. It is the woman who carries the royal bloodline. My husband, your Grandfather Amenhotep III, may he rest in peace, understood this. He alone devoted himself to me. Amongst many, I was the Great Wife. He honored me in ways that were unheard of. He built a palace, obelisks, and temples for me—but despite all the love he had for me, he couldn't stop the hatred the Amen priesthood had for our family. And…"

"Amen priest?" Tut interrupts.

"Shh," I whisper, covering his mouth. "They're always listening."

I paused for a moment and stared at my young grandson. My memory is inflicting my feelings.

"Yes, I have to tell you now about your story, and we will begin with the story of your father."

"They especially hated your father—"

CHAPTER FIVE
WAENRE / AMENHOTEP IV

"WAENRE!" "Waenre—"

"Waenre—"

The shouts grow louder. A blurred image of an old man sitting on a mud-brick wall with his elbows on his knees, in deep thought, is revealed. The shouts are getting closer with each passing moment, exposing his details. The foot of a *black* man of brown-olive complexion. A sandal with jewelry on it seam together very well, showing that he is from wealth. His clothes show richness and royalty but are also worn and old.

"*Waenre—*"

He sits there, holding a *gold* staff topped by a *gold serpent*. Looking distraught and confound with thoughts and memories, a sense of comfort and warmth comes over him, as the rays of the sun, beaming down on his head and face.

***

ON (HELIOPOLIS) - CITY OF THE SUN: 28TH YEAR RULE OF AMENHOTEP III

A DISTANT SOUND is coming from afar.

"*Waenre —* "

Sunlight spills through four alabaster columns into a large bedroom and down onto a floor, lowered oversize bed surrounded with huge pillows going around it and shines on my brown-olive complexion face.

The distant sound is identified as the voice of a woman. A gorgeous, younger middle-age dark olive-skinned Goddess enters the room wearing a beautiful white cotton gown and gold accent jewelry showing royalty. She is the Royal Great Wife…my mother…*Queen Tiy*.

"Waenre…Waenre…Get up!" She says, walking into my room. "Waenre…Get up now!"

Twisting and moaning from my deep sleep and the sun rays shining on my face, I wake. Lifting up fast, I turn my entire body to the side facing the entrance while my feet smack the floor—

—I answer…

"Yes, mother…. I'm up!"

I quickly get up from bed, attempting to acknowledge her, but she is quick and to the point.

"How will it look to your father, and the rest of the court that a prince of Kemet is late to his own wedding?" she whispers, walking towards me.

"Late! Damn," I said. "Sorry, Mother." My voice is shaking reluctantly, and my stomach tightens up with guilt.

"It is alright, Waenre. They will not dare start anything without me." She says, hands reaching out to me. "You are still having those dreams?"

Before I could answer, I recognize my younger brother, Prince Semenkhare, walking into my room. The room instantly fills in his sarcastic cheerful presence, all smiles, and concern. His eyes catch mine as I smile, shaking my head.

"Waenre ...you are not ready yet!" he says.
Our mother turns to greet him and walks towards the outer columns outside my room to give the servants permission to enter to prepare me for the ceremony.

Grateful.

When we were younger, the servants had to chase us down the halls to dress Semenkhare and me. I fought all of them because I could do it myself. "*Its tradition,*" our mother would always say to us. The servants always did their duties, never complaining.

Today is a special day, so the preparation is welcomed, while I stare at my mother with a blank gaze.

"Waenre, you know you can tell me anything. What's troubling you?" she asks.

My eyes unreadable, not wanting to give the answers she seeks.

"You have arranged so much for me. I'm not sure I will be able to do the tasks you would have me to do." I replied.

"Your father and I have noticed your growth and your knowledge of the old ways," she says.

"I'm not worried about my duties to the throne. But more so, my duties as a husband. Do you think she loves —"

"Yes," she cuts me off, walking up to me, placing her hand on my shoulder. "I've spoken to her, and there is great love and responsibility in her heart for you." She responds with smiles at both her sons. "I personally feel and understand the love you have for your cousin. And yes, to ensure your inheritance to the throne, I have arranged for you to marry Nefertiti. But all will be well, my son."

My throat tightens. "I have noticed the way she looks at me. I'm sure she knows the importance of this union," I said softly, nodding my head at my brother.

My mother looks back at Semenkhare, then the servants.

"Everyone, please leave me alone with my son," she commands. "Semenkhare, wait outside as well until Waenre comes out."

Everyone begins to exit. Walking up to my brother, I placed my hand on Semenkhare's right shoulder and gave him a nod. As I watch them all exit the room, he turns back and gives me a warm smile and nods in return.

I focus my attention to my mother. She stands there looking at me with silence until the noise of the servants is far in the distance. She walks up to me and places her smooth hand on my face. "Your marriage to Nefertiti is not what troubles you. You are thinking about your father," she utters.

I let out a deep breath and stare off into a dark corner in the room. My mother pulls my attention toward hers. I did not want to get into this with her at this time, but she also wasn't going to leave until she gets a response.

"You are thinking about him—" she continues.

"Yes!" I said, pulling my face away from her grasp. "I know he has grown ill, and I don't want him to think that I'm trying to take the throne from him at his time of weakness. This joining between father and son, I think it will be good for the people. When I first came here from our home in Zarw, I was just a youth, and while playing childhood games, I was paying close attention. Now I'm older. He, well, we've grown apart."

"Your father is very proud of you, Waenre," my mother responds. "He just believes in the old ways and thinks that changing any part of it would not benefit the people."

The more my mother speaks, the more I come to realize she does comprehend what I'm genuinely feeling about this. *The old ways are dead.* I want to change it all.

"Mother, you also said that the old ways are dead and that we need something to unite us. The priest *must* listen to our demands... Right?" I said, pacing the floor.

Silence—

I look at my mother; for a moment, I almost forget that I'm about to marry Nefertiti.

"Waenre, we have talked about this before. You are Pharaoh, you are God's son, and this they must accept." She answers. "Don't do this to yourself. You must prepare for today. It is your time now—"

"I just want to make him proud..." My voice grows quiet. "He is still my father and Pharaoh."

"I'm proud of you," she says. "That's all that matters."

I walk over and give her a tight hug. She gives me an irresistible smile that carries over to me.

"I love you mother... you are right... It is my time."

***

THE HOUR GROWS NEAR. The whole kingdom and our allies are in attendance. Music from the ceremony fills the halls as he walks beside me, our bodyguards following close behind. I can feel a shiver of indecision running through me, as we come to the entrance of the Noas.

We enter, but the bodyguards do not. They stand guard outside.

The doors close.

There's a lot we have to do if we're going to change it all. For the first time, I'm frightened of him. Will he do this with me, or will he be against me.

An uncomfortable stillness fills the chamber as he stands there staring at me. His eyes cut through my nervousness. The room immediately diminishes with his substantial authority, all influence, and worry.

He is my father. My King. My Pharaoh, *Amenhotep III…*

CHAPTER SIX
AMENHOTEP III

"IT HAS BEGUN, I should have put an end to this a long time ago!" I say to my son Waenre a few moments later after the chamber door closes.

"An end to what? What are you talking about?" Waenre responds with a tremble in his voice, implying he already knows the answer.

"The priest of Amen and their ways," I answered, pacing the floor back and forth, looking at my son, the entrance and the exit of the Noas chamber. "No Pharaoh has ever challenged them."

"For years, things have gone in favor of the Amen priest," Waenre explains passionately. "The people must know the truth of this new energy that I've grown to love."

I stop pacing the floor and walk over to one of the pillars in the room.

"You are right, there is much here that has to be changed, my son. I feel the understanding of the Aten has yet to be explored by the people of Kemet," I say, looking over the inscriptions on the pillar. "Your mother's people have a good understanding of this energy. But before we can teach new ideas, we have to first reteach the old ways," I continued.

Waenre walks over to me. His face with uncertainty and doubt. He looks at me with a quick stare, his eyes not forgiving.

"I don't think I agree father. My people, yes, have some knowledge of the Aten, but even when I was a child living amongst them, they gave it new names and always changed what they felt were laws or rules.

We have to reteach both, yours and mine. Meryre can help. He has been a priest in Zarw, and know very well of the Aten. The Gods of our fathers...well, you know. The Gods are corrupted," Waenre says with conviction.

More questions rise inside me as he finishes, but for now, I hold them back down. I can't begin to understand what he did to change my mind, but the only thing that matters is... he's right.

"Yes, the understanding of Ra and the NTCHR has been lost, but you have to realize that it was not our people that cause this corruption."

Waenre looks at me with a surprise, not knowing that I would be in agreement with him.

"For years among the New Kingdom Pharaohs, there has been great talk about a Son of God...a Pharaoh, coming to undo the Hyksos pervertedness of the understanding of the NTCHR," I finished.

"I have been taught about the Hyksos. How they enslaved and brought the Habiru here, and corrupted our lands," Waenre replies with anger.

— *the Hyksos, the visions of them invading northern Kemet, looting, and burning everything in their path — raping our women and defeating our armies still scars our memories.*

"It was an awakening for our people," I said. "During the *Middle Kingdom*, Kemet was invaded by the Hyksos. This hoard, pillaged tribes in their path as they reached our lands during a time when we were tremendously disunited, and the defenses of our kingdom were neglected. They dominated us for about one hundred and fifty years... we suffered insults to the NTCHR, their way of life, and culture. This period was known as the *"Great Humiliation —"*

"The *Moseid Regime* cast them out, and the *Thutmoside Pharaohs* with the help of the *NTCHR Amen* reestablished Kemet and brought forth the *New Kingdom.*"

As my vision ends, one idea remains to linger through the blackness of my mind.

I walk closer to my son and whisper to his ear. "The secrets of the NTCHR have been kept here for centuries. Even the Hyksos couldn't understand their nature or their knowledge, but the stars don't lie. I believe you are that king that our father's before us foreseen. You will bring back balance and awareness."

CHAPTER SEVEN
SHAHA

THE COURTYARD WHISPERS with the chatter of scribes, initiates, and music from the ceremony as I approach. I'm not one of them. I keep saying to myself as I stand at the entrance. A craftsman by trade working in both the Upper and Lower regions of the empire. I spend most of my days in the towns of Zarw and Ipu but pride myself in knowing all the etiquette of royalty. My best friends Semenkhare and Waenre, always joke me about being different than most of the servants, especially when I'm at the royal palace.

"*Ii-wy em hotep,*" Semenkhare yells to me as I walk into the courtyard rushing to make it through before being seen and stopped by the initiates or any of the priests themselves.

"*Welcome in peace!*" I answered, saying the same back to him as he approaches. "I'm sorry for being late. I want to be at the ceremony today, but you know — Panehesy will not allow me to attend. So I hid by the columns near the entrance of the temple until I saw you or your brother come out," I continued. "How is he?"

"Well...Panehesy gave the Queen and me a strange look today before entering the temple for the ceremony, and Waenre is talking with Pharaoh. He was hoping that you would be here, so I'll let him know that you were." Semenkhare answers.

We continue to talk, not noticing the bald head priest wearing a leopard-skin with a white robe leading two other priests trailing behind exit the temple from the ceremony. The two priests see the servant talking to the Prince and taps the bald man to get his attention.

"Panehesy," the two priests whisper. Panehesy turns to them as they point towards the Prince. He then turns and sees them and clinches his fist and frowns his face.

"Semenkhare!" Panehesy yells from across the courtyard.

The surrounding chatter comes to a dead silence as everyone's attention is on Semenkhare and me. His voice rings through our ears; the sound of his voice reinforced something inside of me as Semenkhare turns to him.

"May I have a word?" He continues, grinning as he walks towards us.

Semenkhare nods to him and leans closer to me.

"What is it with this guy? Every turn we make, he is following Waenre or me," Semenkhare coaxes.

"There are other forces at work here, Semenkhare," I mutter with a frown and anger on my face. "Trust me for now and listen to what he says… But be mindful of your feelings, and speak to your brother about them. I will see him soon!"

I quickly exit the courtyard as Panehesy gets closer to us. His two priests passed Semenkhare without showing him his royal respect or greeting and exited following me.

Panehesy stops walking to watch me leave and then turns his attention towards the prince as he watches him walk in his direction. When the prince is close, he bows his head in respect.

Panehesy lifts his head with eyes growing wide and presses scornfully, "How many times do I have to tell you and your brother to not consort with such people? They are our help and not for you to deal with. Let the district Governors deal with them if there is a problem! And—"

"With due respect Panehesy, I know you are to guide me, but I can't help to notice your level of frustration with Shaha compared to the other workers amongst us," Semenkhare jumps in.

"He is of no concern to you, and…I will not have this conversation with you about this matter again!" Panehesy finishes looking around to the others watching while stepping forward, getting closer to the prince.

Semenkhare steps back, his vigor broken as he looks him up and down and pushes past him to go back into the temple.

***

AS I WALK THROUGH THE MARKETPLACE, there are a lot of farmers and craftsmen trading and selling food and supplies. The smell of barley and emmer wheat fills the area. I approach a farmers' stall with no intent to buy anything but to collect my thoughts.

Panehesy is becoming a problem…

As the farmer starts to sell me fruit, vegetables, and some flax for making linen. I noticed the two priests that were with Panehesy in the courtyard in the distance.

Are they following me? The realization sets in that they are following me when they ignore and push by the people rudely.

But why? I stare at them in the distance as they get closer, uncertainty gathering by the second.

The "why" doesn't matter, the enraged voice rings inside my head after noticing one of the priests pulling out a small dagger, while the other pushes through at a much faster pace.

If I waste any more time, they will be right on me, creating panic and confusion amongst the people.

There, I see an alley nearby.

I walk over, stop at the entrance, and glance over my left shoulder to see if they are following. Walking down a few feet, I stop and lean up against the wall keeping my gaze at the entrance. I pressed my back to the wall and touched the middle of my forehead with my index and middle fingers pressing against the pineal gland, my eyes still fixed on the entrance.

The blood burns in my veins, my breath quickens, still concentrating on the entrance, a brownish-gray like sandy figure walks out of my body. The throbbing in my head surges with the figure becoming more dense and detailed, looking identical to me and walks towards the entrance of the alleyway. The dust is no longer there, and the figure of me is now a fourth-dimensional aspect of myself. It stands there staring at the priest while they are coming down the market street.

When the priest notices him, the figure continues down the opposite direction from them walking at a moderate pace to a dead-end section until the priest is right behind him.

The priest passes by me. I watch them from the distant alley.

The priest with the dagger runs toward the figure while the other priest watches and stands around to lookout. As the priest with the blade is about to strike, I move from the alleyway and swiftly sneak up directly behind the other priest looking out and struck him on the back of the head, knocking him out. The figure/inner-self me just before the priest with the dagger stabs him in his back, vanishes, immediately turning back the same way it came out, to brownish-gray dust.

It passes through the priest as he falls forward from the thrust of the stabbing movement. I stand directly behind him, the sand falling on me like a downpour from a bucket of water. Sweat rolling down my forehead, my skin burning from the reconnection of the dust returning, hard dirt crunches under my feet. I grab him, drag and pick him up and slam him against a wall in a nearby alley.

"Shaha—" he yelled.

"Enough!" I shout, pressing my forearm against his throat. His muscles tense, grabbing my arm for breath.

"I know what you want and what you are trying to do! You all can not stop this one! He is going to finish this...it is already done, It has already been written! Tell Panehesy..."

An emotion passes across his face, something I can't read as I release him. I walk backward, slowly ducking back into the alley where the shadows are thick by the height of nearby walls. The priest closes his eyes tight and opens them slowly, but I am gone... Whispering loudly, I said...

"I'll be watching — "

CHAPTER EIGHT
QUEEN TIY

MALKATA PALACE - PHARAOH QUARTERS
HE LOOKS EXHAUSTED LYING THERE.

I stand at the entrance. Watching. His face is covered with strain while sleeping on our oversized engraved ivory framed bed, laced in gold, and decorated with some of the finest cotton and silks. The very sight of him strengthens my desires. I walked over with a damp cotton cloth and lay beside him. My movements wake him, and he smiles at me.

My husband, my Pharaoh...

He stares at me as I wipe his forehead. "Thank you," he says, sighing.

"You need to rest, my love," I say. "You are doing too much in one day."

"I'm OK, he says. This meeting will be short, besides Waenre is meeting them at the entrance soon."

"Waenre... Is trying hard to be you." I stop rubbing his forehead and sit up. I narrow my eyes, hoping my face is not showing to much emotion. "He's trying to do all the right things, and at the same time, trying to come into his own."

I get up from the bed and walk over to a basin on a table and soak the cloth in water. After ringing out most of the water, I walk back over to the bed and sit down, staring at him lying there as he speaks.

"We spoke openly about his endeavors as Co-Regent. And it's like he is trying to create confusion with the priest," he says as he tries to sit up.

"Have you've forgotten?" I replied, wiping his forehead. "It's been so long ago now, but a young Pharaoh... handsome, secure in his views took a commoner into his harem and against the priest, made her Great Wife."

"Look at me." He leans forward and kisses me softly on my lips. "Yes, and how great you are."

"That's where Waenre gets his passion. He watches and remembers everything. He's always been serious," I said, looking into his eyes and holding his hand. "He has so much on him.

"The burdens...

"The nightmares...

"Waenre is still having those dreams, and you and I both know that we can't keep the truth away about the death of his eldest brother, Thutmose."

"Why would you say that?" He puts one of his hands on my shoulder and the other over his mouth while coughing. "You knew what had to be done!"

My shoulders tighten as he released it. I want to shout. *Waenre needs to know the truth, he can handle it.*

I watch as he gets up from the bed. He walks towards the entrance of the room and stops.

Silence... For the briefest moment, sadness overpowers my emotions and flashes through me. *Why doesn't he see what needs to be done?*

The silence is broken from his coughing. He looks over his shoulder towards me as he walks out. "The time will come for him to know the truth, but for now, everything remains the same."

CHAPTER NINE
WAENRE / AMENHOTEP IV

MALKATA PALACE – COURTYARD

COMMANDER GENERAL AYE, a medium built Nubian, brother to my mother, Queen Tiy, and father to my wife Nefertiti, walk to the steps with his General, Nakht Min leading into Malkata Palace. They see Governor/Vizier Ramose, Priest Panehesy, and two Amen Priest coming towards them. Everyone stands outside. My royal guard and I walk to the entrance. When they notice me, they all get to one knee and bow their heads.

"Rise!" I said, smiling at Aye. "My father wishes to see you all."

They all rise to see me already walking away from them into the central area of the Palace. My father sits on his throne as I approach. I walk over and stand next to him. I can see an unquestionable passion burning behind his eyes. Is this the moment where he announces it, I think to myself. Will they accept his command, I wonder.

The men walk over and bow down to one knee to our Pharaoh, my father.

"Rise!" He says.

"Thank you all for taking some time out of your busy schedules to attend this council." His voice vibrates thick and intense, different than usual. *Is my father hiding something from me, from us*? I stare at him as he continues. "As you all know, we are planning for the *Heb-Sed* Festival." He continues barely, coughing and clearing his throat. "My son will partake in the festivities as well as the rites… in my place."

"In your place," I blurt out. Confused, I quickly lower my head as he cuts his eye at me.

The men are standing, some in confusion. Panehesy and his priest's face tighten… with anger.

"Exactly as I said, *in my place!*" He wrinkles his nose at me with disappointment.

CHAPTER TEN
NEFERTITI

ROYAL SLEEPING QUARTERS – WAENRE AND NEFERTITI

LIGHTS FLICKER down the long hallway from the lanterns on the wall lighting up the corridor. The light revels images, 'the god's words,' medu netjer, of nature... the *NTCHR Ogdad: Ptah, Atum, Amen, Khmunu*, the primordial state of the universe, the four dual-gendered twins: *Nun-Naunet, Heh-Hehet, Kek-Keket, Amen-Amenet* on the wall.

At the end of the hallway are two big Nubian royal guards guarding the outside of a large door. The door to my sleeping quarters.

A room very elegantly decorated with gold and silks. I sit in the middle of it in deep meditation.

It's quiet.

All the daily duties, anxieties, fears, and thoughts of the day are lifted from my mind as I slip into consciousness. My vision reveals the past, the present, and unclear images of the future.

The flicker of candle flames dances along draped silks from the walls. A loud *knock* breaks my concentration, and I jolt back. For a moment, I am unaware of what breaks my meditation. My room is still and silent. I look around, trying to see where the sound came from. A deep louder *knock* resonates through the room. It's only then that I realize that it came from outside my door.

"Come in!" I say out loud, still in my meditation sitting position.

There is no response.

"Come in, I said!" I say again, but louder. I look towards the door waiting for the guards outside to open them. For a while, the only sounds in the room are my heavy breathing of frustration and the dull, soft thumping of my heartbeat.

I get up and walk to the door. Anxious of who is there, I pause for a second and open it slowly.

"Hello!" I taunt as I peak around the open door.

With no response back, I open it up all the way and notice that my two guards are gone. I walk further out of my door to see no one around. Not even in the hallway where it is dimly lit, cold, and silent. My hands grab tightly on the door as I step backward into my room, closing the door in front of me.

"Nefertiti!" a deep voice whispers.

Scared to turn around from the door, I push my left shoulder as close to the door as possible, turning slowly until my back is against it. I tense as an oversized hooded figure appears in the candlelight sitting in my meditation area, its robe covering the whole entire body, including the face, hands, and feet.

Frighten, I reach for the door to leave —

"Nefertiti...please, do not be afraid!" the hooded figure whispers again but a little louder.

The voice is different than anything I've ever heard. It had a strange tone and heavy accent almost unrecognizable to any language I knew. I quickly suck in a quick breath and turn around to face this figure.

"How do you...how do you know my name?" I whisper.

"We know..." the hooded figure paused then continued louder, " We know everything!"

The mysterious figure doesn't even move. Eager to know more, I walk away from the door but keep my back close to the walls creeping to the other side of the room.

"I am a messenger of the Aten. I am what you call a NTCHR! My name in your language is Re-Harakhti." He mutters with a hint of excitement.

Immediately hearing this, I fall down to my knees and put my head to the ground in submission and worship.

"Dear child, please do not worship me! I am not your God." His accent is becoming more of a slithering sound humming thick and heavy, different than the Kemetic dialects I've heard and without a doubt, not human. I slowly lift my head and stare at the darkness within the hood where his face would be. "I am a messenger bringing only a message. Please, stand..." His voice takes a distracting turn.

I slowly rise to my feet as he begins to stand. The messenger stands up to an intimidating height of eight and a half to nine feet tall.

He begins to walk over to me.

I swallow hard and close my eyes.

I'm stunned by the messengers' height, his presence, walk, and voice.

When a loud knock is heard at my door. My attention is drawn to the sound, and I look at the door. It was only for a second, but when I turn back around, he was gone. I searched the whole room, and there wasn't any trace of him. He completely vanished.

Afraid and confused, I run to the door and exit.

***

I STAND AT THE ENTRANCE to my servants' quarters. Unaware of my presence, she stands near a stack of folded silk sheets while folding the last one from an empty basket when I enter.

"Where is my husband?" I questioned.

Startled, she turns around and drops the silk sheet she was folding. "Oh! You startled me," she responds. "Pharaoh is having a meeting, my Lady." She answered.

"Very well, please, go and find my mother." I press.

My servant bows to me and walks away swiftly out of her sleeping quarters and down the hallways of the palace. Not knowing what else to do, I walk back over to my room. I stand at my closed door, scared to open it. I look from left to right down each hallway. The idea that Re-Harakhti will be back in my room waiting for me chills my blood.

I take a deep breath and enter.

CHAPTER ELEVEN
WAENRE / AMENHOTEP IV

— FATHER CONTINUE'S WITH HIS IDEAS about the festival —

— will they respect his decisions —

— if the priests believe I'm going to just stand here and allow their disrespect to us, to our Pharaoh —

"My son, your Co-Regent, and I agree that…" My father says, looking in my direction and then giving his attention back to the council. It takes a moment, but I realize he's not just another voice in my head, and I quickly give my attention back to him. "…the traditions of our past have brought our land and our people wealth, power, and a place where others envy." My father solicits, continuing, "However, In this time of our great power, we will do things a little different." The men onlooking and anxious look at each other, anticipating what's coming next. "Amen has given us great things and peace through our lands. I thank him, but his worship will not be taken place during this festival. All the praise will be to the Aten, The Most High!"

As soon as the words came from his mouth, the priest mumbled and backed talked under their breath amongst themselves. One of the priests looked at Panehesy and stepped forward to be heard.

Despite the circumstances, I noticed Nefertiti's servant walking at a swift pace coming down the hallway. Curious at to what was going on, I walk away from the meeting towards the corridor and stand there looking at her servant and also giving partial attention to the meeting.

My father noticed my quick departure but continued. "You may speak your mind if you wish..." He says to the priests who stepped forward. "but make it clear, I have given great thought to my decision." He persisted.

"My Lord, We..." The Amen priests paused for a second to collect his thoughts, his eyes trained on Pharaoh. "...I am not happy with your decision. The statue of Amen has always been conveyed by boat in our festivals. Since the expulsion of the Hyksos rulers, Amen's growth has accelerated due to the vindication of both power and AmenRa as a protector of both the state and may I remind you...the Pharaoh. He is your father, you are his divine son." He exclaimed.

"Please, do not take my comments and decisions in a negative way. Amen is my father, and I am his son, metaphorically speaking. But there is another that needs to be recognized." My father replied.

Before he could continue, the priests over talks him.

"There is no one comparable to Amen! He speaks through us, and we are not pleased!" The priests shouted.

Aye quickly glances over to me at the corridor, but not before I catch the anger gleaming in his eyes. "Gentlemen, your tone to the Pharaoh is unacceptable. This council was called so that we will be first to hear the changes. Pharaoh does not need our blessings or our understanding of any decision he has made.

"That alone means that because he did consult with us, he has great respect for our council. For years I have watched the priesthood of both schools, Amen and Atum fight about what they thought should or shouldn't be accepted throughout Kemet.

"We are the children of Kemet. The land and its power are the food that nurtures us, gives us our strength and knowledge... And Pharaoh is our father." Aye finishes walking and standing in front of the priests and looking at each man there with a stern face.

My father stands and walks down to Aye and touches his shoulder.

"Thank you for your words, General. But you should not have to remind my priest of their loyalty to the throne." He explains.

Pharaoh turns to Panehesy, eyebrows down, showing frustration.

"I hope your servitude to my son is better than these incompetent men that stand before me and dare speak to me in such a manner."

Panehesy steadies his vision on Pharaoh, says nothing, and bows. Still, even so, I see that there is resentment playing out behind his eyes. The Amen priests feeling disrespected by Pharaoh, because of their divinely ministerial positions turned their backs and their attention away from him.

I take one last look at Nefertiti's servant before she turns the corner at the far end of the hallway and resume my full attention back to the meeting and walk towards them.

No!

I shake my head as anger grows in the space between us. Tradition or not, they don't get my empathy.

"What is the meaning of this rude behavior? You, priests, talk so loosely with your tongues and then turn your backs away from your Pharaoh!"

Panehesy turns to me as I stand in front of him and his priests, eyebrows raised in surprise.

"I am not as tolerant of your actions as my father, so you will respect the decision that has been made." I continued as I move to the center of the meeting area.

"There will be no outside worship during this festival other than the Aten! That is my final word!" I yelled and looked over to one of the Weeb-Priests of Re, Meryre, and nod to him to allow the guards to open the doors of the Main Hall.

The Amen Priests mumble something to Panehesy and swiftly exit. Panehesy looks back at me and, without emotion, walks over. "My Lord, may I have a word with you in private."

"Anything you have to say can be said within this council, Panehesy," I insisted.

Meryre walks back towards us, as the Guards close the door. Panehesy ignoring the others frowned his face at me, and I knew then that whatever he wanted to say, it wasn't to be told in front of this council. He quietly shook his head and stepped backward in silence.

"Very well then, this council is over," I ordered.

The color drains from Panehesy's face. He, along with the other men, except for Ramose, bow and exit the Hall. Ramose, bows, and walk over and stands at the entrance of the Hall and waits.

"My Lord, is there anything else you need me to do?" Meryre asks my father and me.

Pharaoh nods to me and slowly walks back to his chair and sits.

"Yes, there is. First, I want to thank you for your patience during this reconstruction period. You have served the people well in the past, and now I want you to help me bring stability to them with these new changes." I answered.

Unbeknown to us, Panehesy comes in from outside of the palace and enters the room, but remains near the entrance not too far from Ramose. Listening and watching.

"Governor/Vizier Ramose wanted to speak with you." Meryre whispers.

I look over to Ramose, and my expression suddenly changes from a smile to a reluctant straight face. Ramose stands only a few feet from Panehesy, and I could see that these men were still waiting to speak with my father, both or me.

"Yes, Yes, I have been avoiding Ramose lately. I suppose we could talk now." I sighed, whispering back.

"Again, thank you for your obedience, loyalty, and hard work. Please go to Zarw and give greetings to my uncle Anen. I'm sure your family also misses you, so spend some time with them and report back to me in a couple of days.

"Panehesy is here and will keep things in order at the temple."

"Thank you, my Lord." Meryre replies and bows.

I watch as Meryre exits the Hall from the eastern corridor. I look over towards Ramose and gesture for him to approach.

Panehesy stands and waits.

CHAPTER TWELVE
NEFERTITI

ROYAL SLEEPING QUARTERS – WAENRE AND NEFERTITI

BEWILDERMENT.

Confusion.

Fear.

Which emotion should I feel, and what expression should I have when my mother enters?

Looking out the open window, I run through the possibilities as my servant enters my room.

"My Lady, your mother is not in her room." She starts. "Do you wish for me to get the Queen for you?"

"No, that will not be necessary. I will speak to Pharaoh Amenhotep later." I responded, walking away from the window and towards my servant.

"Is everything alright?" She asked.

"Everything is alright. I will see my mother later, as well." I answered.

My servant bows and closes the door as she exits the room.

A breeze flows from the open windows, rousing through the locks in my hair as I walk back to the window I was looking out of when my servant entered.

Gazing out at the many workers working on the temple and the nearly finished stadium for the Heb-Seb. I try to use the working and the preparation of the event to keep my mind at ease. Seconds go by as I watch the door, and the interior of my room, waiting, though I do not know if he will appear again.

If he really did appear.

Maybe I was just dreaming in my deep meditation.

I'm losing my mind—

CHAPTER THIRTEEN
WAENRE / AMENHOTEP IV

"THE MEETING DIDN'T GO AS SMOOTHLY as I planned." My father explains.

I leaned to his side and whispered back to him as Ramose approaches.

"No, but telling them is what we really wanted. The Amen Priest is who really troubles me."

As he approaches, walking cautiously. I couldn't help but critique him.

Ramose, an elder and somewhat proud Governor over Thebes and the northern territories. His small and muscular built always made me wonder why he always dresses understandable and straightforward in the traditional tunic of the Viziers of our past.

"Pharaoh, my lord." Both his hands open to plead with us. "There are important matters I need to discuss with you." Ramose insisted.

My father interrupts him but with a rough sickly cough that grabs my attention. *Is my father's sickness getting worse? Is he hiding something from me as well?* His throat sounds dry. I hope he isn't trying to speak. They will notice something if he speaks now. "What news is so urgent that you need to discuss with me about at this particular time Ramose." Pharaoh questions.

"The Hittites, my lord. They are acting up again, causing some major concern." Ramose answers.

"Major concern to whom!" Pharaoh responds, coughing loudly.

I lean closer to my father, avoiding Ramose's leering eyes. "Are you OK?" I whispered.

I moved a little closer again to my father as he nods to me that he's OK. I can hear it, the closer I am to him. His throat—his throat screams for water.

"They are masquerading themselves for an attack against Mitanni. The King of Mitanni asks for your counsel and help. The Hittites demand back only what was theirs, to begin with before the Mitanni and..." Ramose starts his plea.

Before my father could speak, I stepped in. "This is not the first time this happened, and nothing came out of it. They should be left alone to work out their problems." I interject.

"What?!" Ramose shouts, turning his attention to me. "The Hittites will not stop just there. They are trying to build an empire to compete with ours."

"I do not believe that," I shouted.

Panehesy continues to stand in the back and overhears this news. Not liking what he is hearing, he walks a little closer to hear more of the conversation.

Pharaoh coughs more and more—Ramose looks over to him. Giving his attention over to Pharaoh, he continues to share.

"The Mitanni, my Lord, they are our allies, and they will need our help against the Hittites." Ramose persists.

"They are not allies we need under such incidents," I interject forcefully.

"With all due respect, *young* Pharaoh," he says sarcastically. "I believe they are allies we need."

I can see my father struggling to get his voice. With every cough and clearing of his throat, Panehesy moves a tiny step forward, and Ramose's attention gravitates away from me.

Pharaoh takes in a deep breath and begins to speak.

"The King of Mitanni has already given me one of his daughters, and we have been conversing about his other daughter to be part of my harem as well. So we will not disrespect him that way."

Pharaoh looks at me, shakes his head and nods. Though I had more to say, I knew that he was going to allow Ramose to send aid. It takes me a few moments to convince myself that my views will not be heard, my father continues.

"I have, over the years, built great relations with the King, my son, and our mediation in the matter might be beneficial to both parties. We could see if this alleged claim of the Hittites is true." Pharaoh finishes.

I do not accept the claims, but I do respect my father's decision.

"Was there more news for us that you have Ramose?" I asked.

Ramose, feeling proud and confident steps closer, making eye contact with me first, then talking to Pharaoh.

"Yes, my lord. Two things. The Habiru tribes of the Hyksos are inflicting confusion by raiding the villages of the eastern desert. I think we should step up our military presence in those areas." Ramose answers.

"Military Presence!" I taunt. My patience is running low of this back and forth and with Panehesy moving closer and closer to us.

"The Hyksos have been scattered about for years now. I am sure these are only isolated incidences.

"As you know, most of the civilized Habiru are still citizens. I will not attack their less civilized nomadic tribes. The land near Zarw is home to most of them. So I will speak to Commander Aye about sending his most trusted men to handle any incidents in a calm and respected manner." I asserted, looking at Ramose.

He is noticeably frustrated.

"Is there anything else?" I asked.

Ramose, visibly upset, tightens his jaw. I wait for him to answer, but he doesn't respond. His face defeated — he bows and exits the Hall.

A tiny creak pops from a distance. Panehesy movements are heard and don't go unnoticed.

"Panehesy! Was there anything you wanted to speak with us about?" I shouted.

The moment his name was called, he nervously comes forward. "No, my lords. I wanted to speak with Meryre. Sorry for the confusion." Panehesy apologetically, bows, and quickly exits the Hall.

Beams of daylight peek through the rectangular openings of the Hall above. The Medjay Guards secure the doors and return to their post at the entrance of the eastern and western corridors. I walk over to my father and help him up. His delicate fingers grab my hand, and the other hand reaches for my shoulder. His movements are slow.

"Father, you need some rest. Is this not why you made me Co-Regent so that I could help you with things. You are upset, and the coughing is getting worse."

He looks at me, smiles as we walk towards the corridor.

"Just help an old man to his room."

CHAPTER FOURTEEN
NEFERTITI

ROYAL SLEEPING QUARTERS –WAENRE AND NEFERTITI

I USED TO KNOW IF I WAS DREAMING or having a vision. I would always meditate late at night when everyone in the palace had gone to sleep. I learned as a child to give in to my feelings and feel the energy around me to go deeper within myself. Waenre would join me at times now, but lately, I've been doing it mid-day and by myself. At times I would even have an out of body experience, and I would see the world from the perspective of a hawk. Everything below would be tiny, but the world would be vast and small at the same time. I haven't been able to do that in a long time. I don't know if I can get that deep anymore.

I thought if I gaze out this window and watch the workers and the people do their daily duties, it would bring a sense of peace, calmness, and certainty to me. I question Re-Harakhti's visit was a dream, a vision, or was he really here, in this room.

I'm so in my emotions that I didn't even notice that someone had come into the room.

Someone did. I can smell the oils on his body as he approaches.

"Is everything alright? I saw your servant run down the hallway from this direction." Waenre said, walking over to me.

His deep voice eases me gives me a sense of comfort that I continued to look out the window as he gets closer. He walks up to me and puts his strong arms around me from behind. I rest the back of my head on his chest and smile.

"I had a vision or a visit this afternoon during your meeting," I answered, continuing to look out the window. "The visitor said he was a messenger of the Aten and that his name was Re-Harakhti."

Nervous from what he would say or do, I raise my head and look at him quickly to see his response.

Nothing…

Waenre's face just went blank. Not knowing what to say or react to this news. He devoted a lot of time and energy to the Aten, and he knew better than anyone that Re-Harakhti represented the sun deities. *Why has Re-Harakhti not visited him I'm sure he's asking himself?*

Waenre steps back, turns me around, leans over, and kisses me. Smiling, he replies. "Nefertiti, you are the most beautiful woman in the world, and your heart is filled with love for life and awareness.

"I question in no way your visit or doubt the conversation that took place. I trust you, and I trust your knowledge." Waenre concluded.

Hearing these words from him, sparked a tear from my eye. He took his finger and wiped it down my face and off my cheek. I find myself moving closer face-to-face with him, so I grab him and kiss him passionately. We walk over to the floor, lowered bed, and he sits down at the edge. He removes his top, and his beautiful brown chiseled chest, shoulders, arms, and stomach awaits me.

Standing in front of him, I slip off my silk gown…

His face presses against my stomach as he rubs the back of my calves…

His hand moves up my thighs and hips…

We embrace.

He mutters something while his face is still pressed against me.

"I love you," Waenre mutters, falling back on to the bed with me in his arms.

The moment my feet leave the ground, he rolls me over on the bed. My hair falls in the cotton sheets. I open my legs and pull him closer to me. I don't even have a chance to reply back to him before he takes me.

CHAPTER FIFTEEN
AYE

GOING TO THE EASTERN DELTA to look into the situation that is going on with the Habiru has to be handled carefully. Lieutenant Horemheb and his overachieving First Sergeant Ramesses would be great for the task if they stick to protocol. Though Horemheb's devious and arduous behavior is something of a question, he's my only option at the moment.

I'm sitting writing at my desk when they enter my chambers. I don't bother to look up as they approach. "Lieutenant Horemheb, take Ramesses and some men and go to the Eastern Delta. We may have some problems with the Bedouins of the Habiru tribes."

"It would be my pleasure to handle this for you, Commander. It would also give Ramesses the experience he needs to handle the regiment of soldiers in Nubia." Horemheb responds, smiling a sneaky half-grin.

I look up at them and notice the smirk on Horemheb's face.

"This task I ask of you is critical. Pharaoh has asked for our best men for this journey. I trust you will handle anything that may arise there with absolute professionalism." I stated, walking over to them.

"Yes, Sir!" Horemheb calls out, shoving his right fist into his chest while standing at attention.

I dismiss them and watch them exit.

Horemheb touches Ramesses on the shoulder on his way out, muttering something to him. Resentment is in their attitude as they leave.

I continue to stand for a moment, wondering if I chose the right Lieutenant.

As much as I want to handle this on my own, Pharaoh needs me here, and Horemheb is the best Lieutenant for this mission. However, Horemheb is known to have a delusion of grandeur at times.

We all know that too much blood has already been spilled between the Habiru and us.

CHAPTER SIXTEEN
SHAHA

MALKATA PALACE – DINING HALL
"RESPECTFULLY."

I try to remember the last time I was invited into this room. Panehesy and his priests work very hard to make sure that I never enter this Palace. A thousand thoughts race through my mind as I walk into the room to see Wanere, Nefertiti, and Semenkhare sitting at the table.

"My lord, thank you for inviting me to your table," I said, walking over to them.

"Shaha, please call me Wanere. You've been calling me that for years, no need to stop now." Wanere explained as I approach. "You are like an older brother to Semenkhare and me, and you have been around us since our childhood."

I nodded and smiled, remembering the times when I could walk freely around the Palace and be around the royal family.

Nefertiti stands and walks over to me. "Enjoy yourself," she says, "Wanere, excuse me. I have to meet with my mother."

I watch as he walks over to her and kisses her. "Is everything alright?" Wanere ask.

"Everything is fine," Nefertiti answers, "we've been so busy, I haven't told her the news."

"Give her my love," Wanere concluded, smiling at her as she exits the hall.

Semenkhare and I confusingly both look at each other.

"What news?" Semenkhare asks.

Wanere gestures for Semenkhare and me to join him. "Nefertiti's pregnant," he says, smiling, lifting his hands.

Hearing the news, we all immediately embraced each other and locked arms.

"Wanere, she is beautiful and would make a fine mother," I said, finishing the embracement, "Have you told mother?" I ask, walking over to the table to sit.

Semenkhare and Amenhotep looked at me, puzzled as they sat down.

I catch a glimpse of their faces. A new weight settles on my shoulders.

Embarrassment.

"I mean your mother... the Queen, does she know?" I asked, lowering my head and looking down at the table.

Wanere quickly smiles and answers cheerfully. "Yes, yes, I spoke with her earlier this afternoon."

Still embarrassed, I needed to change the subject to move on past my earlier question and how I asked it.

"I do have some news to share with you," I said to Wanere, "You sent some men to the eastern delta?"

Wanere's silent for a long moment, staring at Semenkhare. I could tell he didn't want to get into this conversation, but he answered anyway.

"Yes, I had Aye look into a complaint about some issues with the Habiru tribes," Wanere answered.

"Aye, sent Horemheb, and he took Ramesses with him," I explained.

"OK! Aye sent Horemheb, and he took Ramesses with him…" Wanere repeated with a hint of a question in his voice. "So what!?"

"Commander Aye does not know what happened, and I'm sure Aye's scribe gave the Commander whatever news Horemheb told him to record." I pressed, looking at both of them with anger and anxiety.

"Wanere, they murdered the entire tribe!"

Semenkhare stares on, not knowing what we are talking about; he is confused.

"What? Murdered? Where? When?" Semekhare asks.

"Are you sure," Wanere responds.

"Yes!" I answered.

"How did you come of this knowledge if the Commander was given a false report?" Wanere smacks his fist into his hands.

Fear of who may be listening, I lean over closer to them. Looking around, I wanted to make sure that everything I'm about to tell them is only heard between us even though I know royal guards are standing near.

"Wanere, you both were raised in the Eastern Delta. You know Zarw has eyes and ears. Some amongst us may do their work and live according to the laws of the land, but they are Habiru and also govern themselves."

"These men must be questioned!" Wanere shouts.

"No," I said to Wanere. "Semenkhare, you spoke to your brother about Panehesy?" I asked Semenkhare.

"Yes, but that happened almost a year ago after Wanere's wedding." Semenkhare answers confused, looking at me puzzled.

"What does Panehesy have to do with this?" Wanere ask.

"He has everything to do with this!" I respond, standing and moving to a seat closer to Wanere. "I believe he is the mastermind behind the Amen Priest uprising."

The brothers sit silent. I can see them thinking and trying to make sense of the information I'm giving them.

I can see that Semenkhare understands the severity of it all. "Wanere, he has been acting weird for years." He adds.

"You know how those Sem Priests act." I pause, moving in closer. "If the people knew what the Sem Priest knew, then there will be no need for them." I implored.

"Yes! That is true!" Semenkhare interjects laughing.

"Seriously," I shouted. "According to their law, only Sem Priests know God, and if you questioned them, then God doesn't like it... So they say!"

"Shaha," Wanere jumps in, grabbing my arm, "if these men are plotting against my family and me, and as you stated that General Horemheb might be in on this as well, then I must confront them." Wanere asserts. For a moment, his eyes filled with the anger of tears. "I am Pharaoh—"

"God has more in store for you at the moment, but your... confrontation will come."

"Aten has more in store for *me*? Wanere asks but also confused at the same time. "What are you talking about, Shaha?"

"Your faith in Aten is strong. And your passion for truth and understanding is what guides you." Semenkhare adds. "I'm sure that's what Shaha is trying to say." Semenkhare finishes looking at me with concern.

"He is right. Think deeply about this, Wanere. When we were children, you were always questioning Anen about the Gods..." I said, agreeing with Semenkhare. "You always had to go research the answers for yourself. That's your destiny."

"What?" Wanere ask.

"To Reform!" I shouted.

A royal guard enters the dining hall and interrupts us.

"My lord, a storm, is approaching."

Wanere stands and acknowledges the guard. "Make sure the people are safe, and indoors and then you and your men seek shelter."

The royal guard bows and exits the hall.

"Shaha, please stay here for the night. It is late, and you may get caught in the storm," Wanere adds.

We all walk towards the exit. We can hear the winds hitting up against the palace walls.

"You can stay in one of the guest quarters," Semenkhare implies.

I clear my throat and look at my friends. They've always been so kind to me despite all the blowback from the priesthood.

"Thank you both," I said, exiting with them down the hall towards the entrance. "I've been out all day, and I do need to relax."

Semenkhare looks at me, smiling. "I will send my bathers to you. Enjoy!"

***

STRONG WINDS BLOW AS A GIANT SAND STORM HITS. It's late. The palace is still and quiet. I could never sleep during these storms, so I like to walk the halls. It is quiet despite the winds. The way the torchlight flickers, it looks like it's dancing to a rhythm as I walk down the hall towards the inner chamber. As I get closer, I can see another light from inside.

In the chamber, the light is in the adjoining room. I tense, keeping still peaking in as a man's voice speaks.

Its Wanere!

This time I catch a different tone of voice in his speech, an accent I've only heard from the older priests. I continue to watch as he places the torch in a holder on the wall and falls to his knees.

"God!" Wanere pleads. "Aten, please give me strength and guidance. I want to serve you correctly and give you all the praise."

I observe as Wanere is encircled by the light from the torch as the darkness smothers the room. The darkness overcomes me as I continue to watch Wanere.

"You are my father, and I am your son, please show me a sign, please..." He continues, sobbing.

"*Wanereeeeeeeee,*" a slithering sounding voice answers him, its speech carrying a different tone I've never heard before.

"Who's there? Show yourself to your Pharaoh!" Wanere shouts as he stands and grabs the torch off the wall.

Within the shadows, a hooded figure moves unnoticed by Wanere, but I can see something moving around.

I keep still and continued to look on.

"I'm letting this overwhelm me," Wanere replies.

The hooded figure moves closer to Wanere unseen as he continues to talk.

"My fathers before me were strong... Ahmose, Thutmose. I ask, please give me the strength of them."

The figure stops and stares at him.

Within the darkness, it stands right in front of him but is still unnoticed.

"For now, the Amen priest will have their way..." Wanere alludes. "For now!"

I continue to watch and listen.

Silence!

When nothing answers Wanere, the light returns to the room, and it's very bright.

"I finally got a response," Wanere replies.

Startled to see me peeking in, he looks up at me. Both in a daze, we had the same look on our faces of not knowing what to do.

CHAPTER SEVENTEEN
THE HEB-SEB

BEFORE TODAY, we celebrated the continued rule of a pharaoh.

Today we honor *two*, Amenhotep III and his son Amenhotep IV.

A Grand Jubilee, The Heb-Seb Closing Day.

A long festive week in honor of the Pharaohs. Foreign dignitaries have come from distant kingdoms. The streets are filled with people and merchants — men, women, and children crowd around openings in the arena to catch a glimpse of the royal family.

"Over here, over here! You can see them from here." A small young boy yells out as he climbs up to a small opening in the arena wall.

A group of boys' run-up as he glances over to them.

"We've been here all week and haven't seen them. What makes you so sure we will see the Pharaohs today?" Another boy from the group cries out. Everyone else in the group looks up at the young boy.

With confidence, the younger boy continued to look through the small opening and yelled to his friends. "Because I'm looking right at them!"

***

AROUND THE STADIUM ARE THE ELITE OF KEMET, as well as foreign royalty. The people feast on prepared meats, fresh fruits and vegetables, baked bread, beer, wine, and honey, as two groups of musicians enter the arena floor and stand along the Grand Processional Walkway.

The first group of musicians is Kemetian women playing their flutes, pipes, harps, and percussions. The second group is Habiran/Asiatic men playing their native instruments.

Sitting not too far from the royal family is Aye and his wife Tey, father and mother to Nefertiti, and Aye's brother and younger brother to Queen Tiye— priest Anen, and his family.

"This is a beautiful day!" Anen says to his wife, Meritamun, as he leans over to kiss her. "The whole week has been beautiful. Tiy and Amenhotep should be proud of their children."

"I agree," Meritamun responds. "I have noticed that Wanere has been rather quiet these past few years. God has blessed him so much."

Meritamun looks away from the musicians and gives her attention to Anen and Aye. "Pharaoh doesn't speak of him as much as he used to do." Meritamun finishes.

At the mention of Wanere, Anen smiles. The curiosity vanishes from Meritamun eyes.

"Don't take his quietness for weakness! We've spoken, and well…" Anen laughs. "Aye, and I rather not spoil it." He presumes, looking past his wife and catching a quick glimpse at the Amen Priest sitting further down from him.

***

A POUNDING OF EXCITEMENT TRAVELS through the arena as he walks in. The Master of Ceremony, a heavy round Kemetian man wearing a black wig with cheek length locks, enters the deep basin of the arena floor. As he reaches the middle of the arena, the music stops.

"Let us first show our respects to our Pharaoh and his Queen!" He yells loudly.

The people stand and look over to Pharaoh Amenhotep III and Queen Tiy and bowed. Pharaoh, looking very sickly, nods. The row behind them sits two smaller girls and Sitamun, a quiet and soft-spoken, daughter/wife to Amenhotep III, who sits cradling Nefertiti's and Amenhotep IV's new baby.

"This is our Royal Family, may the Gods bless them!" The Master of Ceremony shouts.

At that moment the music starts again and the people cheer. The crowd is full, excited, and lively.

Amenhotep IV appears in his divine shining glory sitting on a palanquin, a portable open chair, mounted on two poles, carried at each end on the shoulders of porters. He is proud of this day and holds his head up high with his arms crossed against his chest. In each hand, he holds a royal scepter and, on his head, rests the white crown of Upper Kemet.

Close behind him is his beautiful Chief Queen, Nefertiti, sitting on her covered palanquin. Behind her are three smaller palanquins for their daughters, that are empty.

"She is—" Queen Tiy whispers to herself but turns around to address Tey, who is sitting a couple of rows behind them. "Your daughter is beautiful!"

Touching Aye's shoulder, Tey smiles and responds. "Thank you. Our family is blessed."

"Aten is good to us," Queen Tiy replies, smiling.

Towards the end of the processional march, Amenhotep IV notices the Amen priests. The priests rudely sit there drinking and eating without showing the Royal Family any attention nor respect. Ignoring them, he continues towards the end of the walkway. At the end of the march, four bowmen position themselves along an outer perimeter, each facing one of the four central points.

The porters holding Amenhotep IV palanquin grab firm as he stands and faces his father and mother. The bowmen each dip their arrows in a fire pit beside them and pull back on their bows. Muscles tight and tense. You can see each fiber move through their arms and shoulders as they hold their position pointing into the air.

"These arrows represent our increasing boundaries and our influence on the world!" Amenhotep IV declares.

There is a long pause as they each shoot an arrow lighted with fire high in the air. The arrows soar over the crowd and the people outside of the arena and hit large empty pits that catch flame surrounding the city.

Amenhotep IV locks eyes with the Amen priests who refused to stand and show him and his family respect when he walked in earlier. They look at him with smirks on their faces mocking him as Amenhotep IV speaks.

"May the Aten shine down on us and be the light for the world!" Amenhotep IV concluded.

The crowd roars with excitement and cheer. The arena floors, walls, and pillars shake as the people stomp and scream for their Pharoh. The Jubilee is officially over, but the celebration continues, everyone dances to the festive music, buzzing from the excitement of the demonstration. The royal family joins the Pharaoh and Queen as the people are amused by foreign entertainers. The arena hums with drunken chatter as the sun falls below the horizon. As night falls, the stadium glows with light all over; lanterns hang against the pillared walls.

"You did a good job of preparing this Wanere. The years have been long, but everything turned out the way I envisioned it. You did well." Amenhotep III announces.

Amenhotep IV walks over to his father. "You are my Pharaoh, and I honor you." He says, kissing his forehead.

Nefertiti embraces her daughters, and Queen Tiy stands and kisses her son's cheek. Everyone stares at the arena floor, joining in the excitement of the festivities.

***

THE ROYAL QUARTERS OUTSIDE THE STADIUM. Though the Heb-Seb ends, the music and dancing continue late into the night. Semenkhare and Shaha are sitting drinking wine as Aye enters.

"Any left for me," Aye asks.

"Indeed!" Shaha says.

Semenkhare nods and sips from his canteen, as Shaha reaches over and hands him one full of wine.

"I'm glad this week is over. Wanere had the army on full patrol." Aye explains.

Semenkhare smiles and laughs at Aye. "You have a problem serving your Pharaoh, Uncle!"

"No!" Aye responds, elbowing Semenkhare's shoulder. "Do not say that."

The men all laughed and continued to drink wine when Wanere walks in.

"I'm glad that's over with," Wanere asserts, walking over to Aye.

Aye nods and locks arms with Wanere to greet him. "Someone pass him some wine," Aye requests.

Semenkhare hands him a full canteen.

"Thanks," Wanere says. "That was a long three years preparing for this Heb-Seb. Now I can get down to business."

Before Wanere can finish, Shaha interrupts. "You sure you're ready for the outcome?"

"Yeah," Wanere replies, "I'm sure!"

The men come closer together.

"I'm with you. And the Army, well, they will do whatever I say. So, you just give me the OK." Aye replies.

They all raise their canteens. In unison, they say —

"For Kemet!"

Wanere eyes fill with tears of passion. "For the *world*!" He finishes.

Semenkhare, Shaha, and Aye took the last sip from their canteens and walked out the room with Wanere close behind. Wanere stops at the entrance and looks in the air before exiting. He whispers.

"For Aten, my father —"

CHAPTER EIGHTEEN
SITAMUN

"It is clear!"

Sitting in my room and talking with my mother, Queen Tiy, this morning, I realize that a change is coming. A change I may not be prepared to embrace.

"What's clear?" Queen Tiy asks. "What do you mean?"

"The gods have been good to Kemet. We have stretched further out onto the world. Our fathers would be proud." I replied.

"No, Aten has blessed us." Queen Tiy responds. "Its reach is never-ending."

This is more complex than I thought. The Queen needs to know how I truly feel.

"Can I be honest with you?"

"Yes, of course." Queen Tiy answers back.

"Wanere's, desire to worship Aten may be too much for Kemet," I reply with concern. "The people will never give up Amen and the other gods." My skin prickles as I challenge the Queen. With good attention are my views, but change is hard.

"The people will do whatever is best for Kemet." Queen Tiy replies. "And Aten is best."

"I do not doubt that Aten is best, nor do I deny my faith in God." I swallow hard. I am not trying to offend my mother, my queen. "But all Kemet has known are the many gods. The idea of one God in Kemet may send bad feelings to the priest. Even uncle Anen, he is still a priest of Ra."

My heartbeat quickens. Will she understand my questioning?

Queen Tiy smiles and walks over to a lantern on the wall. She watches the flame move back and forth, admiring its simplicity.

"Yes," Queen Tiy answers, blowing out the flame. "Anen also knows that Ra is just an aspect of the Aten. But I do know where you are going with this. All the gods are aspects of the one. Without the Aten, there aren't any gods.

"Your father, Pharaoh, to me rides the line, and just tries to keep the peace between both schools of the priesthood and the gods." Queen Tiy finishes.

The comment brings a smile and an agreeance to me.

"He has always been the one of nonconfrontation," I reply. "But I do admire his support with Wanere's search for truth and understanding."

"Maybe Wanere will be the one to give us a full understanding of the Aten." Queen Tiy responds, turning and walking towards the exit of my room.

I stand there looking at her before she leaves. *Understanding*? The words creep to the edge of my lips, anxious to escape.

Yet, I said nothing right away.

With a look of concern for my brother, I whispered before she exited.

"I know what I feel, our fathers have taught us to believe in one God, but I see no real difference in Aten's worship."

CHAPTER NINETEEN
WAENRE / AMENHOTEP IV

I STAY IN MY PRIVATE WORSHIP HALL to meditate, learn, and to have peace. I can escape from all the politics of the world and just focus on understanding God's purpose for me. I don't have to face the Amen priests. I don't have to face anyone.

Meryre and two of his young scribes finish their daily duties within the hall. As they exit, I can hear some chatter from outside near the entrance, but I refuse to break my meditation to see what's going on.

***

OUTSIDE THE TEMPLE, CHIEF AMEN PRIEST AWAITS, looking at the colossal obelisk next to it. Meryre sees the priest and whispers to the scribes as they approach him.

"You should be killed, denouncing Amen!" the priest shouts. "He is your God!"

Meryre not wanting to deal with the confrontation tells the two scribes to go on without him. The priest looks at the scribes as they pass him with disgust and anger. When he turns around, Meryre is in his face.

"Look, your Pharaoh is about to come out, and it is best that you have no words with him," Meryre explains.

"My Pharaoh!" the priest says sarcastically. "Please—"

The priest pushes past Meryre. "You think I was here to speak with you," he adds. "You are nobody to me. You're nothing!"

***

MY CONCENTRATION IS BROKEN. All of the yelling from outside pulled me out of my meditation. I come to the temple to get away from all of the noise and bureaucracy. Disappointed, I stand at the exit of the hall, taking deep breaths before leaving the temple to see what's going on.

With a calmness, I exit, Meryre sees me and walks away to catch up with his scribes. I also see Chief Amen Priest walking up to me, yelling.

"Pharaoh!"

"What do you want?" I answered, not showing the irritation that my deep thought and calmness had been interrupted.

The priest grunts. "I need to speak with you!"

"You—"

Cutting him off before he could utter another word. "We have nothing to say to one another."

"Oh! We have a lot to talk about," he adds.
I walked past him and down the steps of the temple.

"You are making some dangerous mistakes!" He implies.

"Dangerous!" I shouted, turning back around to him.

Despite everything in me that wants to punch him in his face, the memory of my father's words to me about holding back and staying strong, I stand, listen, and breathe deeply.

"May I remind you that Amen is the Supreme God of this land and the reason you ever was able to be on the throne. Pharaoh Ahmose would be displeased if he were alive." The priest argues.

"Well, he's not! And I rather you did not talk about my kin like you know them. The Cult of Amen, was, the God of my conquering ancestors that drove out the Hyksos, but It was my Great Great Grandfather Thutmose III who made this Empire!" I contended.

"Amen was his God, was he not?" The priest questioned.

Turning back around and walking down the steps of the temple, I answered. "True indeed, but even my fathers before me seek out the truth, to the understanding of God."

"Truth!" The priest shouts. "Amen is truth, and there is nothing else, only Amen! This, I know for sure."

"You know nothing," I laughed. "I know you are not Amen, and my God is my father, and I am his son."

The priest runs in front of me, yelling. I see my guards swiftly approaching him.

"Blasphemer!"

"The only son of God was Heru and his father, Asar, sits under the rule of Amen, he governs the heavens."

I hold my hands up to my guards to keep them back from grabbing the priest. I walked up and approached him face to face.

"Enough!"

"You crave only for wealth, superiority, and power! You priest, don't teach about God, about truth. You don't give the people, nor Kemet true guidance. You only want control. You want their obedience, not their opinions. You treat them like puppets, and you think you are the puppet master.

You are simply a pawn being played like a game. You think you have control over the peoples' minds, but who controls yours."

"I do!"

Anger swells inside the priest as I stand firm in front of him, challenging every remark he makes.

"You are making a serious mistake!" He yells. "Amen is the resident God of this city. Aten is not a replacement. You are placing both yourself, your family, and the country you think you are ruling in grave danger."

"The country I think I'm ruling?" I reply. "You are done challenging my authority, my power!" *How dare he question my authority, my loyalty to Kemet*? Chief priest or not, he will not disrespect me, my family, nor my rule.

"You leave me no choice," I continue. "You are relieved of your duties as Chief Priest of Amen!"

The priest stiffens.

"What? You can't—"

"I can't what," I cut him off. "I'm Pharaoh. I'm your Pharaoh, and from this day on, every Amen Temple will be closed, Amen's name erased from every wall."

I look over to my guards and gesture to them to take him away.

"Your treasury is now offerings for Aten," I ordered.

The priest is shocked, his eyes narrowed as the guards grab him by his arms, shouting. "You just remember." Resisting, he screams at me once more as the guards carry him away. "All actions have consequences—"

It's at this very moment I realized this fight is not over.

The war has only just begun.

***

THUNDEROUS SOUNDS ROAR through the streets of Thebes. The ground shakes as chariots move through them. At every temple, the priest is met by soldiers. Without hesitation or explanation, they burst in and destroyed every image of AmenRa. Everywhere his name is mention, they erased. They also knocked on every door and announced that there would be no public worship of any Gods in Thebes. Nor will there be any adoration of any of the Gods. All, if any reverence, must be made privately, but Amen is forbidden of any worship, public and or privately.

***

STANDING LOOKING OUTSIDE of my window listening to the cries and commotion from the people of Thebes. Nefertiti enters our chambers. I watch as my beautiful wife swiftly walks towards me.

"Wanere, what did you do?"

"I did what had to be done," I answered.

"Closing the Temples of Amen?!" Nefertiti shouts. "Destroying his image and his name. That's your idea of what had to be done."

"Aten…" I responded.

"Aten, Aten!" Nefertiti continues, cutting me off. "God is no man and doesn't need to show his dominance. You should not put God on our level. Aten is greater than any of that. God doesn't get mad. We do."

At that moment, I knew that I had overreacted.

"Oh, Aten!" I cried out, falling to my knees. "What have I done?"

Nefertiti grabs me to give me comfort. Her hands on my shoulders, squeezing to ease my pain.

"You have to correct this, Wanere. Pharaoh will not approve," she pleads.

"I'm Pharaoh now," I reply sobbing. "Father is sick, and they will manipulate him. This is God's will."

"How do you know?" Nefertiti askes.

I stare back at her with silence.

"How do you know?"

My eyes hang open in an empty stare.

"Wanere, how do you know?" She asked again, grabbing my face looking into my eyes.

"He spoke to me," I whispered.

Shocked by my response, she stares, waiting for me to continue.

"I know because he spoke to me. For the first time, I stopped to listen, and I heard…"

"Me—"

***

THE FEW REMAINING GUARDS leave to the other temples and other areas where Amen's image stood. Sand blows through the city as people continue to roam the streets. Some crying, some angry, and some just confused too what all just happen. Before today, Amen was God; his presence was everywhere. Now, God doesn't have a face.

Commander Aye walks out of the main Temple of Amen-Ra and stands at the front. The priests run out after him. Angry and confused, they demand and audience.

"This temple and treasury are now closed," Aye demands, looking at the priests. "Amen is forbidden. This is Pharaoh's will!

Aye jumps on his chariot and drives off down the street through the sandy wind.

***

A SINCE OF FRUSTRATION LIFTS from my mind as I sit in Malkata Palace courtyard meditating on the events that happened these last few days. A pulse of comfort travels through me as she enters the yard.

"How are you feeling this evening, my son?" Queen Tiy asks, walking over to me.

It's hard to look up at her. I know I overreacted and promised my father that I would push these changes slowly. However, I was left with no choice.

"I'm angry," I answered.

She sits at my side and looks into my troubled face. For a moment, I did not want to continue.

"The corruption of the priests angers me," I argued. "They should be obedient to their Pharaoh and just listen to me."

"You know your father is not very happy with your actions," she says

"Well, I'm not him," I responded, trying to be as polite as possible. "He has a lot more patience than me. He always found a way to win favor over the people to his way of thinking. But he still had the same problems with the Cult of Amen."

"Nothing has changed," I argued, as my mother gets up and paces around. "I had to enforce that change!"

"Wait!"

"Where is my father?" I ask. "Is everything OK?"

Nothing. It's like I'm speaking to the wall.

"Mother…"

"Yes." She looks over her shoulder at me. "Your father, despite everything that has happened and now with his health, added another wife to his harem. The young daughter of the Mitanni King." She added with a hint of jealousy.

"He calls her Kiya —"

I take in the response, processing it in my head.

"Does that bother you?" I ask without showing to much attention to the question.

"No." She answered. "But something just doesn't feel right."

"Hey, let him have his young wife. You're still the Queen." I shake my head ardently, but I laugh, trying to make lite of the situation.

"You and Sitamun finally made peace, let's not start over."

She shakes her head, looking back at me, exhaling a frustrated breath.

"My son, my Pharaoh. I love you, but don't let that same love blind you."

CHAPTER TWENTY
PANEHESY

THE LIGHTS FROM THE LANTERNS flicker down the carved walls as I travel deep into the center of the temple. Golden lanterns hang on the rough stone, lighting the large stone steps in the darkness with its soft glow. As I enter, I stare at Chief Amen Priest and the other Amen priest that are standing in the lit hall. General Horemheb is also standing near a doorway as four men walk-in: Ramesses, and three of the priest's sons.

"Did all of you make sure you weren't followed?" I asked.

"Yes, Grandmaster!" Chief Amen Priest answered. "I was the last to enter. No one followed us."

I nudge Horemheb to fall in behind them when they got to the center of the room. The rest of us formed a giant circle around the men as Horemheb stands in front of them. We stand together, the men in black robes and the four initiates in white. I, the Grandmaster of the society, wore a purple robe spangled with embroidered stars and girdled with a cord of gold.

"The rites you have successfully completed in these last couple of days, purpose, was to test your minds and introduce you to our secret society of wisdom and to show the mastership of natural laws that you may one day use," Horemheb affirms.

I step forward to the center, studying the men that would one day continue the society and grow our group.

"Into this brotherhood, I give you duties, responsibilities, and you are also sworn to secrecy. You are to protect Kemet from any influences," I stated.

The men bow their heads, I turn my attention towards the entrance and continued.

"Outside and from within—"

***

BREATHING HEAVY WITH BEADS OF SWEAT gathered on his forehead. Meryre has found the entrance to the temple. He walks down the large set of stone steps, stair after stair, descending towards the echos below. With each step, he looks behind him before taking the next, afraid that someone has seen him. Quietly he walks down the dim-lit narrow halls to a bigger room and hides in the darkness. From the adjoining room, he could hear the voices of Horemheb and Panehesy.

Chest tightening, suffocating under the threat of being found, Meryre quietly peeks around to watch and listen....

***

"THE ROYAL FAMILY must be destroyed, and AMEN will make sure that this will happen," I asserted, giving my attention away from the entrance of the room and back on the initiates.

"Let the Elite Assassins come forward!"

A camouflage wall not too far behind the men is revealed as the lights from the lanterns shift to show it is there. The room is filled quickly as black-garbed warriors appear from behind the wall.

"The Assassins, Sons of Priests," I shout to the initiates. "And now you are one of us!"

My head lowers when I hear a different sound other than what's in the room. It is quiet, muffled, and sounds like a beaten drum. Yet I recognize his presence to know who it is.

"I can hear you," I whispered.

Meryre's heartbeat quickens as the initiates, and all in the room fall prostrate in submission. Witnessing it all, he falls back fearful and runs in the darkness up the stone steps towards the entrance of the temple. He grabs a lantern off the wall and sprints out into the darkness of the night, looking back at the temple to see if anyone is following him. Seeing no one there, he turns around to continue back to the palace, when suddenly I am standing in front of him.

Meryre stops running immediately, dropping the lantern in the sand. Surprised and confused, he desperately tries to talk.

"How?" Meryre says. "Panehesy, how did you get here?"

Meryre bends over, resting one hand on his knee to catch his breath and the other hand reaching out for me grabbing my robe.

I pull out a dagger from the front right pocket of my robe and grab Meryre's hand, pulling him closer.

"You don't think I sensed you when you entered the temple," I taunt.

"What?" Meryre asks.

"You had to follow them," I continued, holding Meryre as he tries to fight and pull away. "You had to keep digging your nose into business that doesn't pertain to you!"

My grasp is too strong a hold for Meryre.

"Why?" Meryre yells out, trying to fight the dagger away from him. "Why are you doing this?"

"Because there is only one God," I reply. "Amen, he is Lord!"

Meryre eyes bulge and inhale a sharp breath as I frantically stab him several times in the gut. Blood splatter is everywhere. I take one last thrust of the dagger into him and pull out, pushing him away, watching him fall to the ground. The light from the lantern is fading. The red drops of blood turn into black splotches as the flame dies out.

I close my eyes, wiping my face off of his blood.

As I stand there in the darkness, one whisper persists a word teetering through the emptiness of my mind.

"Forgive me."

CHAPTER TWENTY-ONE
WAENRE / AMENHOTEP IV

BACK AT THE PALACE LIBRARY, I try to hold on to Nefertiti's words, allow the palace life to fulfill me the way it did my father. Balancing politics and family is something he is good handling. I made an effort to socialize with the members of the royal family, my father and mother, Sitiamun, my father's new Mitanni wife, Kiya, Tey, Nefertiti's mother, and Nefertiti and our three daughters: Meritaten, Meketaten, and Ankhsenpaten. Servants enter to serve us wine, bread, and fruit.

"This is a beautiful morning," I emphasized. "A morning without the negative chatter of the Amen Priest."

Pharaoh struggles to pick up and sip wine on his own. Sadness grows inside me as I watch him clear his throat to speak.

"The conflict has been made by both sides, my son, and I'm sure you will hear from them again." Pharaoh conveys.

My daughters, Meritaten and Meketaten, play with my mother and my sister Sitamun. They take gold lace beads and string it on a turquoise line of cotton. Seeing them both working together and playing with my daughters almost makes me forget all my problems.

"Both sides?!" I whined.

"There is nothing wrong Wanere, showing your love for God, I support your actions," Queen Tiy soothes.

Pharaoh puts down his wine and sits up in his chair. "Who else agrees with her?" Pharaoh asks, clearing his throat. "Speak your mind."

Silence as they all look at each other quietly. Nefertiti looks at me while holding our youngest daughter, Ankhsenpaten. Conflicted, the look on her face has as she walks over to her mother, Tey, handing Ankhsenpaten to her.

"I agree," Nefertiti says.

Kiya, my mother, Sitiamun, and my father all look at her.

"I agree with him, and I support my husband."

"There were times when I had questions, but his logic made sense."

My father, Pharaoh, emotionless, sits there quietly.

"My Lord, if I may," Kiya responds. "I have something to share."

Kiya sits, waiting for Pharaoh to respond. He looks at her unresponsive with a blank stare.

"Please speak your mind," I respond, tired of the silence.

"In my land, God is also one, and at the same time, many," Kiya adds, looking around, intimidated by the group, yet confident in her delivery. "He has many attributes. I find it rather honorable that you have such a strong love for your Creator. I support you."

Pharaoh forces a nod, though he cannot bring it to himself to speak.

Nefertiti looks at the Queen and her mother and back over to me. *Surprised.* It put a smile on my face, though Kiya doesn't even look my way.

Nefertiti walks over to pick up Ankhsenpaten when we are all interrupted by a servant.

"My Lord," a servant franticly, walking in swiftly. "My Lord, it's—"

Before he could finish, Panehesy walks in the room covered in blood carrying Meryre. Panehesy, crying lays Meryre down in front of us. Meryre's body is covered in blood, and his robe looks like tattered rags. His dark skin blistered from the scorching sun, stained by the dirt and sand singed into every wound. He looks like he was butchered, dragged, and left out in the blazing heat.

"I found—" Panehesy starts but falls to the ground crying. "I found him like this..."

"Found him where?" I yelled, running over to Meryre's lifeless body.

Sitamun and Tey take the two remaining girls as she, Nefertiti, and Kiya exit the room. Nefertiti looks back at me as I fall to my knees, holding Meryre, crying over him.

My eyes follow the bloody cloths up to a crying and sorrowful Panehesy.

"What happened to him?" I ask. "Who did this?"

"My Lord, I found him behind the Temple of Amen-Ra." Panehesy accuses.

My father struggles to his feet and walks over to us.

"Meryre was killed by Chief Amen Priest," Panehesy indicts.

The servants exit the library as more of the royal guards come running in.

"Thank you, Panehesy, for bringing him to me," I tremble with anger. "Please leave us."

The guards rushed in, pushing pass Panehesy as he bows. He turns to exit, not before I noticed the bruising on his hands and tears in his robe. I didn't have a chance to study him before his departure, and my father and mother, rushing over to give me comfort.

"Let the servants take him Wanere," Queen Tiy requests. "He needs to be prepared for burial."

"No!" I yelled. "I will take him!"

Pharaoh grabs me around my waist and shoulder. "Son, please!"

Servants enter and take Meryre's body. The royal guards are put on high alert for Chief Amen Priest. As my father gives the order, I leave and exit the library, passing Nefertiti walking in.

"Where is he going?" Nefertiti asks.

My heart is pounding with anger walking out. I can hear Nefertiti and my father talking as I exit down the hall.

"To see the High Priest, I suppose," Pharaoh answered. He calls two of the guards over when all the servants' exit. "Go to the Amen Temple and bring my son back here. Do whatever is necessary to bring him back, just don't harm him."

The guards bow and exit.

***

THOUGH I AM DRIVEN BY ANGER AND VENGEANCE, I push forward as the thundering sound of my chariot speeds down the street towards the Amen temple. Through my rage, tear-filled vision, I see Chief Amen Priest standing at the front of the Temple as if waiting for me to arrive. His hands lift in the air, face smiling with a huge grin from ear to ear as I approach. With a firm grip, I pull the chariot to a sliding stop kicking up sand and dirt everywhere.

Jumping off the chariot, I run to him.

"My Lord, My Lord, I am glad you are here," Chief Amen Priest asserts. "I wanted to apologize for my behavior to you the other day and also how I treated priest Mery —"

Before he could utter his name, my fist smacks him right between his eyes. The force cracked his nose, oozing blood down his hands as he grabs his face falling to the ground.

"Shut up, you murderer!" I yelled. "Don't you dare say his name!"

Chief Amen Priest looks up at me, spitting blood from his mouth. "Are you mad?" He asks. "What are you doing?"

So caught up with my rage, I had not noticed the few people that were nearby and several of the priests coming out of the temple.

"You know why I'm here," I yelled, standing over him. Sweat dripping down my face and back. "You killed my priest, you took his life from him, now, I will return the favor!"

Chief Amen Priest is desperately trying to scoot away from me when I grab his neck with one hand and continuing to punch him with the other. He is kicking and trying to overcome me, but he is stunned by the punching to his face as he gasps for breath.

I can hear the distant roar of chariots approaching. Chief Amen Priest, does not attempt to fight back at this point as I continue to choke and punch him. A gasp slips from his mouth. Then his body went lifeless.

Four royal guards approach and jump off their chariots and run over to us. Amen priests and people gathered around when I took my last punch, dropping his body to the ground. Pushing past the crowd, the royal guards grab me, pulling me away. Every muscle in my body tenses; blood falling from my hands, all anger and vengeance removed.

"Get off of me," I yelled! "I command you to let me go!"

Helpless against their strength, the two guards say nothing but stand there holding me. A bystander runs over to check the priest. He stands and looks at the group of Amen priest that has gathered, then over to me.

"He's dead!" The bystander shouts, lowering his head, catching his breath. "He killed him!" Pointing at me, looking at the people and the Amen priest. "He killed a man!"

The Amen priest rushed over and surrounded the dead priest, as more guards pulled up and pushed them back to clean up the incident. The crowd begins to get unstable and resist the guards.

"Wait for the violent outbreak if you want, but we should leave." My voice breaks.

The royal guards escort me to the chariots and back to the Palace to be seen by my father.

***

I INHALE ABRUPTLY as the guards usher me in the Malkata Palace main throne room. The closer I get to them, the frustration builds on my father's face, the more I don't regret taking the priest's life. My mother's eyes bulge, seeing my hands and clothes covered with blood splatter.

"What did you do, Wanere?" Pharaoh asks.

"I did justice," I emphasized, pulling my arms away from the guards. "I gave him back to his false God!"

In disbelief, my mother stares silent, shocked by my response.

"You killed the man!" My father yelled, raising his hands to the guards to back away from me.

"Yes," I responded with no reservations.

"Wanere," Pharaoh complained. "You have disrespected this council and have broken the law."

The law, the law.

"The Law," I stated. "We are the law!"

Pharaoh stands and walks over to me. "You have a lot to learn, my son," he implies. "I must show justice as well because if I don't, then this throne will never be under our rule again."

My mother stands but remains at her throne. "Why don't he just leave for a while, maybe go to Memphis," Queen Tiy interjects. "A brief stay in the northern capital and a visit to the Eastern Delta might give you a different perspective."

"Memphis would not be much different from here, but it is a way I can reestablish trust and loyalty from the people again," Pharaoh added, shaking his head at me. "And fixing the mess you have made."

Before I can respond, he continues.

"After the preparations are made, you must leave Thebes and not return unless I send for you," Pharaoh continued.

"Yes, father," I replied with resentment.
Pharaoh walks away from me and back to his throne. "Your mother will accompany you," he insisted.

My mother narrows her eyes, looking at him, but he does not look her way.

"My daughter will stay. Kiya and Nefertiti will join you and the rest of your court," he asserts. "Also take some of the Habiru tribe that are still in Thebes. They were leaving to go towards Zarw. You might as well escort them out."

Coughing, clearing his throat, Pharaoh's voice strains, and my mother stands speechless, looking at him. "I will say nothing more about it, I have spoken, and it will be done."

With that, he turns, slowly walks to my mother, and kisses her cheek without saying a word.

He's really forcing me out. Forcing us out.

"Mother, please let's get ready to leave," I whined, walking to her.

My mother, the queen, her face is flushed, eyes filled with tears. We slowly turn and walk away from him.

In the distance, we hear him coughing as servants rush to his aid.

CHAPTER TWENTY-TWO

AYE

AFTER MANY DAYS OF PREPARATION, the journey to Memphis begins. Young Pharaoh and his family board the Royal Vessel. Shaha and Semenkhare accompany them as fifty other boats are stretched on the Nile ready to leave. Everything that has happened has left resentment in the eyes and hearts of many Kemetians. However, a lot was inspired by Wanere that I agree with. In the distance, Pharaoh sits with his guards and nursing servants at his side, watching. I watch the laborers board loading equipment, livestock, and the rest of the royal baggage into the vast hulls of the wooden vessels. The army stands watching and protecting us all during this transition.

The army had its moments of disagreements as well, but I still have the loyalty of the men. Horemheb and his men watch when I approach him, as the few remaining crew and people board.

"Horemheb, stay and keep the city protected while I'm gone," I instructed. "Half of the men will be here with you, and the other half will leave with me. Ramesses will take command of the chariots surrounding the city."

I lock eyes with Horemheb, who bows to me and turns his chariot around, riding off with Ramesses and five of the soldiers.

"Peace be with you and may God bless you," I shouted.

"Nakht Min, have the rest of the soldiers board the vessels," I commanded. "I will be in the first vessel with the Royal Family.

Wanere waves to me from the Royal boat. I secured the few remaining tribes boarding and waited for the final word to sail from the captains.

Boarded, I watch the crew finish the preparations to leave as I walk to the main hull.

I swallow hard and take in a deep breath.

I look at Wanere on the bow with his hands in the air, face gazing at the sun, praying.

Watching him, it's very convincing and assuring to believe in him and know we'll be alright.

I take one final look at my home.

We cast off —

CHAPTER TWENTY-THREE
WAENRE / AMENHOTEP IV / AKHENATEN

FRESH AIR FILLS my lungs. My heart sinks as we drift away from Thebes, a feeling of great burden weakens me. I press my palms against my side to hide my trembling hands when my wife and daughters come to the bow to join me. I sit with them, showing no signs of defeat and pain. Capturing the beauty of the land around us as my two oldest daughters Merytaten and Meketaten, climb up on my lap, and the nurse hands the youngest, Ankhesenpaten, to Nefertiti.

My mother, Queen Tiy, joins us and sits in a comfortable chair next to us. Kiya, knowing that Nefertiti dislikes her around me, enjoys the view from the back of the boat.

The first few days pass quickly. The vessels are operated by thirty oarsmen as they glide swiftly down the Nile. Navigators on each boat constantly test the depth of the river with long hollow poles.

Feeling better than I did days before, I try to enjoy the journey to our new home. In my quarters, Nefertiti is getting dressed nearby.

"I'm glad we left Thebes," I mutter, sipping on wine. "How do you feel about us leaving?"

"Wanere, I'm glad," Nefertiti answers reluctantly.

"Come sit with me," I ask.

Her beauty is something to admire. Her radiance is beguiling as I watch her walk over to me. Looking into my eyes, she sits on my lap and kisses me. Her hands slide down my back. Her touch makes me want to burst; it's even too hard to focus on kissing her back. Her passionate kiss moves from my mouth as she pulls away and grabs my wine.

"I want more children," she interjects, sipping the wine. "A son maybe. You do need an heir."

Caught a little off guard, I had to agree with her.

"I was just thinking about that," I replied. "More children would be nice. A son even better."

Nefertiti presses her forehead against mine. "That's great, I was really hoping you would agree with me." She leaned down and kissed my bottom lip very softly. Pulling away from my lips slowly, she holds on to my mouth for as long as she could before letting it go. "Wanere…"

Heart racing, face flushed. She knows how much I want her. How our passion for each other takes our intimacy to a different level. The softness of her touch, the tone of her voice, I close my eyes as she pulls me in.

"Yes," I whispered softly.

Lifting her nightgown up to her thighs, dipping two fingers into the wine. "Hmm…" She moaned. She takes her wet fingers and rubs on her breast, leaving the wine dripping down the middle of them. "Come here and taste your wine, come here and taste me."

Our eyes locked on each other. Our heartbeat sounding as one. I pull her to me, breathing heavily, grabbing her by the waist. I kiss her chin and move my mouth to her neck. Her faint moaning, her body quivers when I take her in my mouth.

***

As the moonlight sways onto the Nile waters, everyone on the royal vessel has retired. The other boats are quiet as well, but for the one carrying the army, music is being played as the men dine and dance with the servants. I sit with Shaha on the deck of the royal boat sharing with him poetry I've been writing when something in the distance catches my attention.

"Shaha," I shouted with excitement.

"Yes, Wanere," Shaha replied.

Noticing a bright light towards the mountaintops, I point to the northeast at an intense glow near the horizon.

"What do you think that is?" I ask with curiosity.

Shaha stands and walks closer. He looks back at me with a blank stare. I'm not sure if it's a look of fear or curiosity.

"I don't know!" Shaha answers.

For a moment, his stare stalled me too. It was unlike any light I've ever seen. Too bright to be from a tribe or settlement and furthermore, to high up to hold any large encampment.

"Stop the boat," I commanded, yelling to any crew that was around. "Stop the boat!"

"Wanere, are you sure?" Shaha asks.

"I guess—Yes, I'm sure."

The captain orders the crew to stop and gave signals to the other boats to do the same. Aye, runs out onto the deck. Half sleep but giving full attention to me as he approaches.

"Pharaoh, is everything alright?" Aye asks.

"Yes, everything is alright," I answered. "Get Nakht Min, and meet me on the ground. We will camp here for the night."

"Yes, sir."

Hesitating to walk away, Aye stays at attention. "Please give us time to check the area before you come over to land. I want to secure it."

I look over at Shaha, who is standing waiting. I'm so anxious to get off this boat and set up camp that I'm not allowing my men to protect us.

"Very well—"

Aye rushes off and grabs a small squad and one other from the boat nearby and takes two longboats of men to land.

"Shaha, go wake up my brother," I insisted. "Have him get my mother, Nefertiti, and Kiya as well."

Shaha bows and exited the deck. I walk to the side of the boat. Aye, and his men are already on land. I can see their lanterns moving about in the distance.

Moments later, my mother walks up to me while I watch the lights dance in the darkness.

"Wanere..." She calls.

"Everything is OK mother, we are stopping here for the night."

Before she could ask more, I turn around to her and smile. "Everything is OK."

"OK," she replies.

"It's time we gave everyone some space to themselves. We will sail off in a day or two. I just need to check on something come daylight."

My mom, always so positive and understanding. Her heart is so pure. She doesn't say a word but smiles and walk over to Nefertiti and Kiya as they walk up to the deck.

One of the longboats sailed back and gave the assurance that it was safe to sail over.

The longboats from the other boats all sailed over, leaving but a few crew and guards behind to maintain and watch the anchored vessels. On land, the servants set up the royal quarters, and the remaining crew, along with the army, set up tent areas for the other people with them. There are three hundred tents in total, but the royal quarters are as big as twenty tents by itself, section off into smaller quarters, leaving a big area for Nefertiti and me.

Despite the large glow in the distance atop the mountains, no one commented on it. I'm not sure if they can see what Shaha and I can see, but everyone takes to their temporary living space without any confusion or problems.

For now, we sleep.

***

THE SUN RISES INTO THE VALLEY. I exit the tent to see that before me to the east is a vast expanse of barren land. Beyond that, a range of low mountains forming a cliff at one point. Amazed and inspired by the landscape, I look in the direction of the lights from the night before. Semenkhare and Shaha exit the tent, not too long behind me.

"I couldn't see all that last night," I explained.

"See what?" Shaha ask.

"All of this," I answered with excitement, pointing to the land and the mountains.

Aye, and four of his men walk over to us.

"Let's check it out," Shaha adds, looking at Aye and me.

"Check what out," Aye asks.

"Grab some men and horses," I asserted.

Shaha points to two servants in the vicinity. They all walked over to one of the horse areas and started to attach them to chariots.

"I saw something last night over there, behind those groups of mountains in the distance," I responded. "Did you see the lights, It lit up most of the sky."

"What lights?" Aye asked, looking at Semenkhare as Shaha and the servants walk back towards us with the chariots.

"Yeah, what lights?" Semenkhare asked as well. "I didn't see any lights... The moon, yes, but no lights behind any mountains."

"I saw it."

Shaha's voice is barely a whisper, like he didn't want the servants seeing him conversing with us, but Semenkhare and I heard him.

"Semenkhare let my mother and Nefertiti know that we are going to scout forward awhile and then come accompany me, Shaha, and Aye." Semenkhare nods and goes off to give them the news. The servants also were relieved to go finish their daily duties.

"Wanere, Aye, look at the way the sun is rising," Shaha says.

"This must be a sign," I said, staring at the distant mountains where we will be riding too. "There is a break in the mountains that sort of resembles the symbol for the horizon."

Aye desperately tries to see what Shaha and I are seeing, but I notice that he's just being supportive.

Semenkhare walks back to us, and we all mount the chariots and ride off. Kiya comes out watching us leave as well as others from the tents. I have instructed officials that still serve me to serve Nefertiti because she will keep things in order while I'm not present. While the rest of Aye's men surround the perimeter of the base camp to keep them all safe.

***

FOOTHILL OF THE MOUNTAIN, we stand looking for a way to the top. We had to have been riding now for hours to get just to this point. The terrain wasn't that tough, but it looks like we've still gone up really high. I stand on the hill at the bottom of the mountain, turning toward the direction from where we came, I can see a speck of smoke from our camp before the ridge.

"Semenkhare, Aye, you and your men stay here and keep watch," I instructed. "Shaha, you come with me."

"Pharoah, if I may," Aye interjects. "Let me send a couple of men with you to go ahead of you, at least, to make sure it's safe."

"It is safe, Aye," I assured. "Trust me, It will be alright."

Aye bows and looks at Shaha. Shaha nods at him and Semenkhare.

"I will watch him and protect him with my life," Shaha adds. "We will be careful."

"We need to move," I say.

"May Aten be with you," Semenkhare affirms.

"Aten is with us all," I reply.

Shaha took the lead and saw a narrow trail we could take that wasn't too dangerous. It wasn't wide enough for chariot nor horse, and the gravel was so loose that it almost became slippery in some areas.

We climb the rocky mountain taking each step very carefully as the others watch from below. I can see Aye pacing back and forth, talking to Semenkhare. He means well, I know. My safety is his biggest concern, so I'm sure he's fussing about me doing this without him and his men. Rest assured, we can see a wider pathway up ahead.

"Hopefully, this pathway will take us all the way up and to another path going all the way down around the other side of the mountain when we return," Shaha says.

"I agree."

"I've been thinking Shaha —"

Slipping a little from the loose rock, Shaha reaches back and grabs my hand, pulling me forward.

"I got you, Wanere."

"Thanks!"

"Shaha, the way the sun rose earlier was special," I emphasized. "I mean, a warmth came over me, but I'm not sure what." For a moment there was silence between us, I wondered if Shaha really saw that light last night, or was he just saying he did. It doesn't matter now, he's here with me, and I can see a glow ahead.

Sweat drips down my face, my breath is heavy when we finally reach the top. A large empty flat surface and nothing around but a couple of small shrubs was all that was up here.

"Where's the light?" Shaha asked.

"I don't know," I answered. "So, you did see it."

"Yes, I did," Shaha replies. "It was very bright. You don't think it was just the way the sun was shining up here, do you?"

We both walked around, trying to make sense of the size of this plateau in comparison to the mountain. It just doesn't make any sense.

"Nonetheless, let us give thanks to Aten for this safe journey," I asserted.

We prostrate for prayer and meditation when we hear a faint, humming sound. The sound had structure and made the ground move. The loose rock around us was lifting off the ground. Terrified, we look up to see a bright light coming down from the sky.

***

AT THE BOTTOM, the men sit and wait. Semenkhare and Aye are concerned.

"What the hell was that?" Semenkhare ask.

"I don't know," Aye answered. "It came from the top."

They all look up to see a bright light from the top of the mountain. Aye being a solider, immediately starts to climb with his men, and Semenkhare follows.

When they reached the top, they see Shaha and I holding our hands to our face protecting our eyes from the strong glare of the light above.

"Wanere!" Semenkhare yells.

"Pharaoh, don't move," Aye shouts, "We are coming towards you. You and Shaha, don't move!"

Heart racing, the light felt like heavy bags of sand weighing us down.

"I can't see," I cried, "I can't see anything!"

The men desperately try to get close to us as the bright light descends from the sky. The closer the light got to us, the more dirt and rock would lift off the ground. The wind is swirling, pushing around us, as small bushes and foliage catch on fire. They burn without burning, staying lit, creating light on the ground.

A high pitch sound rings through our ears when a huge figure appears from the bright blinding light and piercing sound, taking away the hearing and sight of the men except for me. They fall to their knees, holding their ears, screaming.

"I can't see!"

"I can't move!"

"I can't hear anything!"

"Pharaoh!"

My whole body flinches when hot air hits me like a brick to the face. Looking at my men, my brother, I am frozen with fear. A tall humanoid being wearing an oversize hooded cloak step out from the light standing to what appears to be nine feet in height. The sight overcomes everything inside me, removing the strength to stand as I fall to my knees. Lifting my head slowly, I look into the blackness of the hood to see yellow eyes starring back at me.

"I am a messenger of our God, Aten, be not afraid," The stranger says with a hissing sound dialect unrecognizable to anything I've ever heard.

Frightened, I look away, seeing that the others are motionless, heads to the ground with blank stares on their faces, like in a trance.

"Wanere, look not away from me," The stranger stresses, "I am here. You know who I am."

Slowly looking back at the stranger, my throat burns with the fear of screaming. I am speechless…

"I am… Re-Harakhti," The stranger explains.

My thoughts slow.

No.

No.

My mind seizes at the notion.

"You're not Aten?" I forcibly ask.

"Yes, and no," Re-Harakhti answered. "I am Aten, just as you are, Aten. Aten is within everyone and everything. It is just a name, a name we choose to use for the Creator."

"No!" I close my eyes, recalling the conversation I had with Nefertiti about him. She was right. She has been right about it all.

"Why are you here?" I ask, starring back into his yellow eyes, "What do you want from me!?"

He takes a step towards me.

Tears burn behind my eyes as I fall prostrate before him. Clicking sounds from the bird-like talons of his foot draw near my head as he stands over me.

"My King, Amen, is planning a military coup against you and your family!"

"You must not return to Thebes," he explains.

"Amen, he is real?" I whispered.

"Yes, all the gods are real, but we are no different than you," Re-Harakhti answeres, "We all praise the Divine Creator Aten, and seek its love."

Re-Harakhti extends his hand to help me up as the tears fall down my face.

"Amen, desires to be worshiped. He also feeds off human energy and takes away part of your human souls every time you give this to him."

In disbelief. I shake my head. I have been told about some of this growing up, which pushed me to seek the truth, actually seeing and hearing this, gives this all-new meaning.

"Mentioning Amen after your prayers will strengthen him. He will manipulate you into thinking you are praying to something or someone else, as soon as you end your thought, prayer, and or statement, uttering his name, he grows stronger. Amen is not even his real name. You humans gave him that name.

"Aten, Amen, and many other names used for God is just a name given to symbolize its unseen presence. The very idea of a God is nothing more than a concept you humans created for yourselves, an abstract idea, nothing more. Aten, the creator, needs no worship. The only worship is of self. Build temples to honor the greatness within yourself. Pray to yourself, meditate to yourself. Aten is within.

"Aten's greatest creation is life, and to understand the knowledge of creation, is overstanding nature."

Despite the feeling of betrayal, a smile breaks through my anger. A burning desire to know more displaces my frustration.

"I don't understand," I said.

Smiling and moving closer, Re-Harakhti stretches out his empty hand and closes it, making a fist. He reopens it, revealing a tiny seed. "The seed of a tree produces another seed…

"The essence life-form of that tree is also contained within that same seed —"

"So, what you're saying is that Aten is me, and everyone else at the same time," I ask.

I look away, trying to make sense of it all.

"We are an expression of the consciousness of the Creator," Re-Harakhti continues.

Maybe this is the truth I have been seeking my whole life. The questions I have been asking but could never get the answers too.

"Aten is me —"

Nodding with understanding. "I sort of knew or felt something within me at times, but couldn't quite understand what it was."

The realization of this is overwhelming for me and brings me to my knees as the world spins around me.

"It will take patience and commitment to understand all of this," Re-Harakhti asserts, "Our kind have received this knowledge many eons ago during our own evolution, and some of us still feel the need to manipulate and hide the truth."

"The gods, the Netjeru, NTCHR!" I stated.

"We are many, yes, but we are not the Creator," Re-Harakhti says, walking back towards the light. "Aten, the name we chose to use for the Creator, is the force behind the NTCHR, nature... behind us all."

I find my balance and step closer to him as he continues to walk towards the light. "If this is so, then why do we feel the need to worship anything at all?"

"It gives you all comfort and hope, nothing else," Re-Harakhti answers, and looks back at me. "But there is nothing wrong with that. Just know that Aten is one, and you are one with Aten."

He takes his large hand and points to the sun. "Humans reverence the sun, but Aten is that force, the *power behind the sun* —"

"Wanere!"

"Pharaoh..."

Re-Harakhti's voice shifts, steeling everything inside of me and stops me from moving a step closer to him.

"I've come here again to warn you about Amen," Re-Harakhti stresses, "I cannot protect you from him. I come only to give you insight."

"Nefertiti, your wife —"

"She will give you beautiful daughters, and she will love you unconditionally, but your father's wife, the Mitanni Princess, will give you a son. He will be the anointed one. He is the one we have been waiting for."

"A son," I say with confusion, "With Kiya, but Nefertiti..."

"Seek counsel from these men, they will protect you from what's to come," Re-Harakhti interjecting, pointing to the other men kneeling near me. "Because of your faith and your trust in Aten, your name will forever be Akhenaten - *He Who Serves The Aten*."

I look at my men, Semenkhare, Shaha, Aye, and the others, still stuck in a dazed consciousness. The light behind Re-Harakhti shines brighter, blinding me. I fight to mask the bright glare keeping me away from looking at him as he moves towards it. I rub my eyes to regain my sight, turning my gaze to the vicinity he was standing only to see that Re-Harakhti is gone. In that instant, the others also regain consciousness.

"What happened?" Semenkhare ask. "Where is the light?"

Aye runs up to me to make sure I am OK. "Wanere, who was that?"

Aye's men mutter amongst themselves.

"I am OK," I reply.

"Yeah, I blinked, and the light was gone," Shaha said. "What happened?"

I move around the area in search of him. The burnt ground and vegetation was back to its original state. The wind is calm, and the rocks still. Only but echoes of his knowledge imprinted on my mind.

"It was Re-Harakhti," I answered.

The mutters from the men continue until Semenkhare shouts, "Re-Harakhti was here?"

I step forward, pointing to the area the bright light was at. "Yes, and he shared a lot of information with me. He has inspired me to do something that should have been done a long time ago."

They all remain silent for a long moment. Waiting for me to finish. Everyone stands still. But Semenkhare crossed his arms with an expression of disbelief.

"OK, what you are trying to have us believe, is that a God came down in bright light and talked to just you," Semenkhare pressed. "Only you, without us seeing it?"

Shaha, looking at Semenkhare with sharp eyes. "Wanere, and what is that, what should you have done a long time ago?"

I continued to look around at my men, locking eyes with Semenkhare. "Yes, brother, Re-Harakhti was here!"

Semenkhare immediately nodded and bowed with an apologetic expression.

"I will build a new home, a capital city built here below this mountain," I continued. "I will call it Akhetaten –*The Horizon Of The Aten* and I Akhenaten will be the High Priest and Pharaoh to God, Aten!"

"Akhenaten," Semenkhare whispers. "You are changing your name?"

To Semenkhare surprise, I smile at him. "Yes, meaning, He Who Serves The Aten. That is my service."

Standing in the middle of them, turning around so that I can talk to them all. "Brothers," I say as delicately as I can, "you will be my new council and my trusted supporters. I will give each of you new tasks here so that when we return to the camp, my instructions will not be judge by others."

Silence.

"Do I have your loyalty?"

In unison. "Yes, Pharaoh. Our allegiance is to you!"

The men walk in towards me, closing the circle.

May God watch over us.

CHAPTER TWENTY-FOUR
SEMENKHARE

THE MALKATA PALACE stands grand as the sun rises against the horizon on my once home, entering Thebes. The military presence is much higher than it was when I was last here. Groups of men are positioned at every corner, leaving no building unprotected. My heart beats so loud I can hear it over the chariots as I ride in the gates of the palace with fifty men, each with a set of instructions from Akhenaten.

I wait in the great hall to speak with Ramose and Panehesy as guards patrolling the palace walk in and out, checking on me.

Strange.

My father is nowhere to be seen. Not even his servants have come out to greet me nor give me any updates on him.

Guards crowd the corridor entrance of the hall, preventing anyone from entering. I can hear someone ascending the stairs outside the hall. Ramose walks past the guards and approaches me with a boorish look on his face. Two of my men step forward, but I nod to allow him closer.

"I have news from Akhenaten," I said before he could speak.

Ramose takes a moment before speaking, then replies rudely. "Who is this Akhenaten?"

I let out a long, slow breath, trying desperately not to be rude. "He is your Pharaoh, and he has given us instructions in order to prepare the build of the new capital, Akhetaten."

"Wait, where is my father?"

The guards at the corridor turn around and stare at me.

"Your father is ill," Ramose answered. "Shortly after you left, he collapsed and has been on bed rest ever since."

"Wh-what?!" I pressed.

"Then, who is in charge?"

"Me, of course," Ramose reply, with a grudging look on his face, "but Panehesy is looking over the local problems, while I have been...cleaning up the mess your brother made."

"Good!" I emphasized. "You can start by relieving yourself from your duties."

"What?!" Ramose shouts.

It all pours out of me at once, the confidence, the attitude that has fueled me all day waiting. "Yes—" I start, "orders from your Pharaoh Akhenaten, and since my father can't make any decisions at this time, Sitamun with Nakht Min's council will oversee things in Thebes until Akhenaten decides differently."

"You may leave now," I continued, pointing towards the corridor.

Ramose rudely walked off and ordered the guards at the exit to leave, slamming the door of the palace entrance behind him.

Nakht Min enters, passing Ramose on the way in.

"You know your orders," I say to Nakht Min as he approaches.

"Yes, my Lord," Nakht Min walks in and stands before me. "I have already ordered the cessation of all ongoing construction projects. The resources for the construction of the new city is on its way. Praise Aten."

I nod.

"Yes! Aten is great!"

***

MALKATA PALACE FRONT ENTRANCE, my men and I prepare to leave. I have four guards standing by with orders not to allow anyone to approach me since Ramose, and I are leaving on conditions he does not agree with. Panehesy is quick to force his way up to me.

"My Lord…"

"I heard you wanted to see me?" Panehesy moves and stretches his neck around the guards blocking him.

"Yes," I answered reluctantly. I'm never in the best mood when talking to Panehesy. "Your Pharaoh, Akhenaten, request your help in building his new capital."

"You're speaking about Amenhotep?" Panehesy reply with confusion.

Even though I can tell he already knows about Wanere's name change, I do not entertain the explanation.

"Yes, Akhenaten, and he wishes your presence—"

Silence.

The uncomfortable silence between us last but a moment. The frustration in me is building.

"Now!" I stressed. "By the way, the priest of Amen is no longer needed and may return to their regular duties."

No matter what I said, Panehesy would not show much emotion about anything I said. He is very calculated. I'm sure something bad is to come with this order from my brother.

Panehesy stares at me with a blank stare.

"As you wish, young Prince."

CHAPTER TWENTY-FIVE
PANEHESY

"MY LORD, WAIT!"

I push through the door of my quarters, my scribe behind me. He stops by the door when I do not answer him. Urgently and with much frustration, I prepare to leave Thebes with Semenkhare and the others.

"Do you want me to leave with you?" My scribe asks.

Every other remark and comment that I want to make leaves as the only one that matters finally comes out.

"No. Let Horemheb know what is going on," I answered, giving my full attention to my scribe. "He knows what has to be done."

"Yes, my Lord," Scribe reply's back, with an unfamiliar look of desperation in his eyes.

"Wait!" I shouted before he exits.

"I will tell Horemheb myself."

***

I ARRANGE TO MEET HOREMHEB AND RAMESSES at nightfall in the Amen Temple before leaving Thebes. When I enter the temple, there are only a few of my trusted priests standing around listening to Horemheb. I move towards the men with the allure of a high priest, unbeknown to them that tonight is my last night among them.

"Our only duty is to serve Amen," Horemheb explains to the men, nodding to me as I stand next to Rameses.

Stepping forward, I interject. "Our self proclaimed Pharaoh, who has changed his name to Akhenaten, has angered the Gods. Amen will not protect us if we follow his leadership!"

"We have been making progress, before this so call Akhenaten, closed our temples. But we still have a ways to go if we are going to be ready —" Horemheb continues.

As Horemheb continues to speak, a strong wind comes through and blows the torches out. When Ramesses light a lantern, a very large hooded mysterious figure is standing in front of us. He grabs Horemheb, and violently throws him to the ground.

It is one of Amen's messengers. This is strange because they have never revealed themselves to anyone but me.

Our faces heat, growing warmer as he walks around studying us. With every step of his taloned feet scratching the rock beneath it, our ears would ring. The men turn away, avoiding looking at him, but the messenger locked eyes with me and approaches.

"I have a message from my Lord," Amen messenger hissed, "He is disappointed in you all. Has your leadership gone weak, that you can not influence the people?"

"The Pharaoh has cut us off from the people," I explained. "Our temples are closed."

Horemheb, holding his shoulder in pain, crawls over to the other men.

The Amen messenger cut his bright yellow eyes at Horemheb. Rameses, Horemheb, and the others lock their gaze to the ground, fearful of lifting their heads.

"What do you ask of us to do?" I ask, "Our praise is to Amen, he is our God."

The air seems to thicken as we wait to hear a response. The men fell to submission when he hissed.

"Kill him," Amen messenger whispered, walking to a dark corner.

All eyes turn to me, and my stomach dropped.

"Kill Akhenaten!" Amen messenger hissed.

My legs nearly collapse when he vanishes within the darkest corner of the temple.

"I submit!"

CHAPTER TWENTY-SIX
QUEEN TIY

THE CITY OF AKHETATEN under construction with our vast camps in the background, slightly lit from the moons glow. The large mountain towers us like a rock palace, casting its shadow upon us. The chatter and music from the people throughout the encampment create a familiar sound I know all too well. Sitting, watching my son stand with his hands spread out in front of the table of city drawings, planning, and praying, sets me at ease.

"Mother, I'm seeking your council," Akhenaten contends, tears collecting in his eyes. "Our family has worked hard to bring the two lands back together. Within a short period, I have just divided them."

I reach out and grab his hand. "Wanere, I support you. Our ancestors went through rough times in building this dynasty, this legacy." I wipe away the remainder of his tears falling on his cheek.

"You need to be strong," I say. "Don't regret anything. Everything happens for a reason. This was destiny. You made a choice, and this is the path that you chose."

Wanere smiles, but it only lasts a second. He walks away from the table and walks towards the entrance of the tent. He looks out to the people, then looks to the stars and turns back to look at me.

"I took away and denied the engraving images of Kemet from the people because it brought nothing but confusion," Akhenaten says with anger. "These gods of Kemet are not God's at all!"

This weight Wanere bears on his shoulder threaten to break him. I just want to comfort my son and give him the council he desperately seeks. Yet this new narrative that is playing out makes my heart feel heavy in my chest. I think it is time he knows the truth. The truth that his father and I have been withholding from him.

I leave the table and stand by his side. We both look at the people. We listen to their laughter and chatter. Their songs and their whispering prayers. I hold his hand and stare at the night sky.

"I agree," I say, gazing at the moon. "The sun and the cosmos are the real power behind all life in the universe. It was the will of Aten that chose you to spread wisdom and understanding."

"Do you really believe that mother?"

"Yes, I do. Be at peace for right now, you have been chosen, and the Creator does not make mistakes."

"Wanere —"

"I've overheard one of the servants talking about you today."

Wanere looks at me. I can see him from the corner of my eye as I keep staring at the sky.

"What did they say?" he asks.

"I don't remember everything, but your name is forbidden to be spoken in Thebes."

I try to look away, but he grabs my face softly to meet my eyes.

"Some feel that you are still the true heir of Kemet," I continued.

He lets my face go and walks back into the tent.

"I am the true heir. They know the truth, right?!"

I turn around to face him. The moonlight against the back of my head, creating a shadow stretching into the tent towards him.

My face shows of sadness for a moment, but I hide it.

"True... but there is another."

CHAPTER TWENTY-SEVEN
SHAHA

WITHIN AKHENATEN'S TENT, I WATCH HER, Nefertiti, as she meditates on the floor. She hears a noise inside that breaks her concentration. Getting up and walking over to the entrance of the tent, she looks around but sees nothing.

"Oh God," Nefertiti says, afraid to turn around to see what is in her room.

"Re-Harakhti, is that you?"

"No."

She turns around slowly to see a figure standing in the center of the room.

She turns slowly to see… me.

"Nefertiti."

My voice barely above a whisper, I call to her softly, so that the guards outside her tent would not hear.

"Shaha!" Nefertiti voice cracks. "What are you doing here?!"

"Where is Wanere?" I ask, speaking softly, covering my lips with one finger, then shushing her.

Nefertiti stands there, confused, looking at me. I swallow hard, not sure if being here is the right time. *I made a promise to her that I would reveal the truth*, I remind myself. For a moment, I contemplate whether Queen Tiy new that all of this would happen one day.

"I do not understand why you are here, Shaha," Nefertiti emphasizes, pointing to the tent's entrance. "I think you should leave before Wanere, Akhenaten, your Pharoah, comes in here!"

"Please," I beg. "Nefertiti, please, I have something to tell you."

Nefertiti shakes her head and walks towards the tent entrance.

"I'm not who you think I am," I said softly.

She stands there, shocked and confused. "Who are you?"

"I am Wanere's brother," I said with conviction, "his older brother, Thutmose."

"His brother!"

"Thutmose died along time ago."

I can tell the words aren't enough. *I have to show her.*

"No, cousin," I said, standing in front of her.

She stares at me. I close my eyes as the tears fall.

I smile and open them, revealing the yellowish tent and round, elliptical pupils.

"I am alive—"

CHAPTER TWENTY-EIGHT
YOUNG PRINCE TUT

AKHETATEN, ROYAL COURTYARD, EVENING. My throat dries when she stops mid-sentence. Still sitting with her back against a chair, my grandmother, Queen Tiy, leans forward. With a small smile on her face, she just looks at me.

"Why did you stop?" I ask.

"Why did you stop with the story?"

My mind aches for more. The voices of everyone hum through me, waiting to be revealed.

"I don't understand..." I mutter.

"Shaha is Thutmose?!"

Confused, looking for answers from my grandmother, she just sits there smiling at me.

"His eyes," I stated. "Tell me again what happen to his eyes."

"You want to know the rest?" Queen Tiy asks.

I cling to her question, nervousness choking my throat, anxiously getting the words out. "I want to know. I want to know everything!"

Before she could speak, I hear footsteps approaching. Thinking it is one of the servants, I did not turn around right away. It was not until her eyes flicker as tears fall down her face that I turned around and saw him.

Shaha, walking towards me.

Wearing the royal uniform of a Pharaoh.

In his hand, he holds the Double Crown of Upper and Lower Kemet.

"You want to know the rest of the story?" Shaha asks.

"The story is not over, young Tut."

"Your story has only just begun."

EPILOGUE

MY EYES ARE SHUT tight. I try to have an open mind when they tell me the news. I don't believe it. I open my eyes slowly, but I want them to close. Afraid of the truth or just afraid of what I'm seeing and not gazing at the yellow hues and black pupils starring back at me.

She walks over to me speaking, but my ears are ringing, and no words are coming out of her mouth. As the realization of all this starts to take hold, I can feel the low moan escaping from my mouth.

"Thutmose!"

As soon as I yelled his name, I collapsed forward, falling on her as she approaches. Their faces looking over me: Nefertiti and Shaha.

"Shaha, what are you playing at?" I manage to speak. "You look nothing like my brother, Thutmose—"

"I'm alive, Wanere," Shaha assures me. "You were very young when It happened. Pharaoh and our mother did everything in their power to save me, and it worked."

With their help, I stood up and walked over to the table to sit. I sit with my arms leaning on the cold wood of the table. Nefertiti sits right beside me, rubbing my back.

Remembering the brother from my early childhood. My brother, the priest that took me to the sacred temples, flows through my mind, as I brace myself for the questions I'm too scared to ask.

The yellow tent in his eyes is now fading back to the opaque white color I have been used to seeing.

"Save you from what? What happened to you, and why did they hide this from me?"

Silence…

His stare at Nefertiti sinks a sharp pain in my chest.

"I will explain everything to you," Shaha explains. "To you both."

Nefertiti takes her hand off my back and immediately grabs my hand. The pain from my chest drops down to my hand as she takes hold of it.

"For now, we have to prepare for his coming," Shaha asserts. "The essence that is inside of me that brought me back from death will be the same power that will give him life."

"Who?" Nefertiti and I said in unison.

"Your son!"

For a moment, Nefertiti and I didn't know what to say. How do you respond to all of this?

Then she enters my tent.

AUTHOR'S NOTE

WHEN I THINK OF YOU, Asia, I shed many tears. Twenty years ago, you came into my life and unlocked the doors I locked within myself. This began my journey to seeking *TRUTH*. This was when I learned the truth of Kemet and my ancestors. I shed tears when I wrote my first sentence that turned into a script that later became this novel. And while you, the reader, hold this in your hand now, I shed tears again as I did so many years ago.

While the characters in this novel are highly dramatized, they were real living people, and the impact they have left on this world is still being discovered, learned, taught, and an inspiration to many.

Pharaoh: The Power Behind The Sun was originally written almost twenty years ago during a time when I had hit the lowest experience of my life. I felt angry, afraid, and vulnerable to the outcome that was given to me. After my loss, everything that I knew to be "*TRUTH*" was not, and the comforts of *HOPE* was empty. I was eager to learn but, more importantly, becoming aware that real truth is of the *KNOWLEDGE OF SELF*. What started out to be the writing down of notes from research with my twin, that turned into a script, which evolved into this novel, along with the many sleepless nights of sadness became the one thing that fulfilled and rebuilt my confidence.

One of my goals besides writing and publishing this novel is that if just one person would read it and have their hearts, minds, opened and changed. Then I would be doing something consequential against the pervertedness and lies that are still being taught.

A goal completed, and this book exists, and *you* are reading it.

I am truly honored and humbled, thank you.

If this story, the characters, the symbolism, or any parts of the book affects you in any way, then I ask that you do not let it just stay within the words of this book. We all have the power to change, and awakened to a deeper understanding of self, awakened to the *DEEP SLEEP* we are in.

The evidence is all around us. I call out to our ancestors and ask for continued guidance. I honor them and give praise to the Almighty. Practice *MA'AT* in your daily life: Truth, Justice, Harmony, Balance, Order, Reciprocity, and Propriety.

We have been told untruths and knocked down for far too long. I close using the ancient word...

ASE` (It is so...)!

ACKNOWLEDGMENTS

THE ALMIGHTY and the ancestors have blessed my life and brought people into my life. Thank you for everything you have done.

My wife, Monica B., thank you for sacrificing everything to give me the opportunities I have always been able to dream and create. I am truly and forever grateful for your unconditional love and support all these many years. Thank you for giving me my *"Baby Girl,"* who has been the inspiration for me taking that *leap* into the learning of SELF. I miss her very much, but she lives in our love for each other. Monica, you had believed in me, in my research, in my script and my book before I was strong enough to write my first sentence. My rock, my early draft(s) reader, my partner, thank you for being my biggest supporter, and for pushing me when I wanted to stop and was too scared to finish. *I LOVE YOU.*

My three sons and best friends, AJ (*Antoine Jr.*), Jaden, and Asa, my purpose to all that I do. You have also pushed me and believed in me throughout the years. Your random mentioning of how far I got, or which chapter I was writing at the moment, kept me writing more and more every day. Thank you for sitting around the table as a family and reading the final draft and giving your approval of its completion. Thank you all, and I love you very much.

Before going forward to other members of my family and friends, I must take a moment, even shed some tears with a smile for my first best friend ever in life, my brother, my twin, Spencer R. Holmes. Bro, this would not be possible if not for the research you have done with me, and the many nights we stayed up and created the story. From the early times back in VA when we challenged all that we knew to seek out the truth despite the foundations that were already ingrained within us. Thank you for making such a selfless sacrifice, you put your heart and your creative mind into the script that helped me tell the story I wanted to tell. Get ready, Book Two: The Son, is our co-author moment.

Mom and Dad, thank you for your support all these years. Dad, you introduced me to know that there is a Creator. All those late nights of lectures and debates we had in the kitchen sparked my desire for learning. You taught me to never settle, to never give up, and always finish what you start. I love you, and I know Big Mom and Big Dad are with the ancestors and are watching over us every day. Mom, my first teacher of knowing the power of unconditional love and the first person to introduce the Almighty's love for me. You are my Queen Tiy, always protecting, loving, and supporting me in so many ways, I love you. I know Granny and Granddad are also with the ancestors and are watching over us every day.

Also, special thank you to the cousins, aunts, and uncles who pushed me during my childhood and the ones that challenged my mind as an adult.

My sister, Monica L., my muse for wanting to write and read book after book until my eyes hurt. You are a great example of poetic excellence and wordsmith. Growing up, we would watch you join book clubs at school and admire your passion for reading. The way you allowed the words to pull you into its world. I never knew how amazing that experience would be like until in college when a friend gave me a book that forever changed my life. Sis, thank you for your unconditional love, and I love you, always.

My other parents, my in-laws, thank you for your continuous support. You both have loved me from day one and embraced me as a son. I am forever grateful for your guidance throughout my adult years of life. I always call you by your names, but you are also Mom and Dad to me as well. The first readers of my early, early drafts of the book. Thanks for challenging me to be better. I love you.

Reis A., Rob R., Dana D.(cousin), Spence(cousin), David A.(cousin), Buddy, Chris Irby(RIP), Troy S., Corey A., Antoine T., Junie S., Earl O., Thurmond A., Tony L., Jeff B., Flex A., Carl P., K Rob, and Kevin W., you guys are such wonderful friends, best friends, and brothers that I am blessed and grateful that I had most of you all growing up, within the last fifteen years of my life and that I still have you all now. All of you have encouraged, push, challenge, and motivated me throughout the years. Words cannot express how I feel about each and every one of you. I can write another book about all the adventures and discussions we have all had. Thank you for loving me unconditionally and allowing me to become the man I am today. I am glad to call all of you, my *"Brother."* I love you. To my many friends and family whose name I did not mention, who helped me along my journey, you too are very important. You know who you are and how I feel about you. Thank you.

To my many teachers who have taught me through their online lectures and many authored books, thank you for helping me discover, *ME*, and what I want to say and write. Special shout-out to Anthony T. Browder, Dr. Ray Hagins, Dr. Yosef Ben-Jochannan, John Henrik Clarke, and Professor Kaba Hiawatha Kamene.

I saved the best acknowledgment for last but *certainly* not least: to my readers. All of this would not be possible without you. Thank you for allowing me to take you through an adventure into ancient Kemet. There are thousands of stories waiting to be told and rediscovered. I look forward to continuing the journey with you.

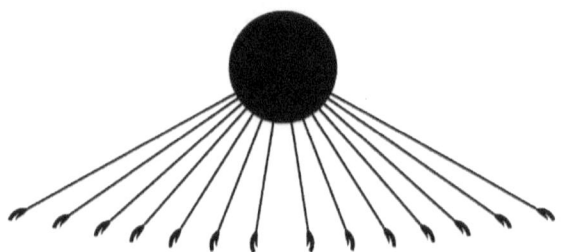